Courage
for
Beginners

Courage for Beginners

by Karen Harrington

LITTLE, BROWN AND COMPANY
New York · Boston

Little, Brown and Company

Hachette Book Group
237 Park Avenue, New York, NY 10017
Visit our website at www.lb-kids.com

Little, Brown and Company is a division of Hachette Book Group, Inc.
The Little, Brown name and logo are trademarks of Hachette Book Group, Inc.

The publisher is not responsible for websites (or their content) that are not owned by the publisher.

First Edition: August 2014

Library of Congress Cataloging-in-Publication Data

Harrington, Karen, 1967–
  Courage for beginners / by Karen Harrington. — First edition.
    pages cm
  Summary: "Twelve-year-old Mysti Murphy of Texas wishes she were a character in a book. If her life were fiction, she'd know how to solve her problems at school; take care of her family when her dad has to spend time in the hospital; and deal with her family's secret: that her mother is agoraphobic and never leaves the house" — Provided by publisher.
  ISBN 978-0-316-21048-5 (hardcover) — ISBN 978-0-316-21047-8 (electronic book)
  [1. Agoraphobia—Fiction. 2. Family problems—Fiction. 3. Middle schools—Fiction. 4. Schools—Fiction. 5. Texas—Fiction.] I. Title.
  PZ7.H23816Co 2014
  [Fic]—dc23

2013021596

10 9 8 7 6 5 4 3 2 1

RRD-C

Printed in the United States of America

For Chloe and Molly

It takes courage to grow up and become who you really are.

—e. e. cummings

chapter 1

I don't know much, but I do know people stop to look at unusual things. People slow down to look at car accidents. People pull out their cameras to snap pictures of orange sunsets. People lie on the grass in the dark if a news reporter says you might spot a meteor shower after midnight.

Maybe I look unusual right now. I probably do, but then, how could I stop to look at myself? That would be a trick.

I could be a painting in a museum. *Girl Who Sits by a Window.*

Museumgoers in colorful summer sandals would walk by my picture frame and say, *Here is an odd red-haired girl sitting by her window. What is she waiting for? What is she looking at? What are we looking at?*

In school I learned that if you are really quiet, people will think you are smart. This is another trick. I'm not smart. I just can't stop thinking.

I sit here motionless and still. Thinking. There is nothing else to do.

Most people aren't stuck inside their boring houses all the livelong day.

I am. That alone makes me unusual.

Dad is at work and Mama is in her room with the door closed and I have no idea about Laura. Mama just painted her walls Seafoam Green in preparation for another mural, and I wouldn't want to be in there if I was her, because of the fresh paint smell. But Laura is probably sidled up next to Mama on her bed, discussing whether the new mural should be a tree or teddy bears at a picnic or teddy bears at a picnic under a tree. As for me, I told Mama to quit changing the mural scene on my wall. I'm just fine with her version of the *Mona Lisa*, which we call the *Faux-na Lisa*. So far, she's left it there. She is starting on a forest in the hallway. For once in my life, I'm thankful none of my friends come over. Actually, that my one friend doesn't come over. There is only one. But I would die a thousand deaths of embarrassment if he saw all Mama's paintings. A portrait of Sponge-Bob is displayed over the hallway toilet. How do you explain that? Maybe it's just another unusual thing about my life.

The thing to do is move away from the window and stop looking at the street. It's getting hot, and I can already tell this August afternoon is going to be a heat-down, beat-down. It's my turn to water the backyard vegetables. They are probably screaming for me now. *Help! Help us!* If vegetables could scream, that is. But I have to wait for Woman Who Goes Somewhere to walk by our house. I need to take her picture and solve the mystery of where she is going before I get in trouble again.

Around the Fourth of July, I'd gotten the grounding of my life for taking pictures of Woman Who Goes Somewhere. Every flip-flop day of the summer, this woman has walked past my house, slow and steady and always in some weird outfit. Long baggy pants. Neon-yellow shirts. A parka! Let me tell you this: No one in Texas needs a parka. Nothing about this woman says she's a professional walker. And I know what they look like. There are two power walkers on our block who wear black-and-green warm-ups and put their hair up in tight ponytails. That is what they are supposed to do. Not Woman Who Goes Somewhere. Her hair is usually wild and disorganized. She doesn't carry a purse. She doesn't have anyone with her. She strolls to the beat of her own music. Where is she going? I have my theories. There are a lot of things going on in the big, wide world. Dangerous things. Adventurous things. Unusual things.

So I took some pictures of her with my camera. Big deal. I sat still as a statue at my windowsill one morning and waited for her to flip-flop past. Then, *snap*. I took two pictures. They didn't turn out too bad considering there is a screen covering my window. Unlike the Jenningses next door, we don't have giant trees in our front yard. Just tomato vines and cantaloupes growing every which way because Mama says they need the benefit of the full sun. But I wanted a clearer picture. So I figured out how to unscrew the screen so that I'd have a clear view. If my parents found out, which they did, they would have a cow, which they did.

It took Mama two minutes to tell Dad I was a "voyeur" (which means "one who sees" in French, and I don't know what's really wrong with being a person who sees). I didn't say much during their inquisition. I sat at the dinner table while Mama moved her arms through the air and explained my crime. Dad stared at me. I stared at the blue-and-white place mats. They are so old and faded that they've probably been around since the dinosaur age, too. If dinosaurs used place mats, that is. That is what my mind does when I'm quiet and it thinks too much. It sees dinosaurs eating off blue-and-white place mats.

"And apparently, this has been going on for some time," she says. "There are several photos in her camera."

Stop and imagine the word SEVERAL with a big spotlight shining on it. That's how Mama said it.

S-E-V-E-R-A-L.

I pictured dinosaurs eating a leafy green salad with croutons on our place mats. Of course, the place mats were high up in the Jenningses' trees so that the dinosaurs could reach them.

"This is really incredible, Mysti," Dad said. "And not in a good way. Can you tell me why you thought this was a good idea?"

Here is a girl thinking this was a good idea because the mystery had tugged at her all summer long.

"I guess I was bored," I replied to my parents.

"Can you tell me why this is a violation of a person's rights?" Dad asked in his I'm-disappointed-in-you voice.

"Because the woman didn't know her picture was being taken," I replied.

Here is a girl thinking this is stating the obvious, seeing how the woman wasn't dressed to go to a store, much less to a photo shoot.

"That's right."

I wondered right then if he'd force me to apologize to Woman Who Goes Somewhere. That would speed up the mystery-solving in a snap.

"I don't know when you'll get your camera back," Mama said. *Fine, I have a camera phone.*

"And you're grounded until further notice." *Fine, I don't go anywhere anyway.*

5

"Yes, ma'am. Yes, sir."

Mama said, "When you know better?"

"You do better," I said.

This was the cue that the lecture had ended. As far as lectures went, that one wasn't too bad.

"Okay, go to your room. You may come out at dinner," Mama said. "I'm sure you can find something better to do than take pictures of unsuspecting people."

You might think, doesn't this girl have something better to do every day than take pictures of unsuspecting people?

But of course you know the answer is no. No, I don't. I've read all my favorite books four times. These books are now at risk of not being my favorites anymore. Their suspense is all exposed and the villains are plain as day.

It's summer, and our family doesn't do anything but read and play games and help Mama harvest the cantaloupes from the front and backyard gardens in the summer. You would think we were a family from out in the country, but we aren't. We are a family three blocks from Tom Thumb, where you can *buy* cantaloupes.

There are odder happenings at my house than home-grown cantaloupes. Stranger things. For one, I like to imagine I'm a character in a book. It makes the long, boring days go by faster.

These are the characters in my book.

There is a person who paints and cooks and never leaves the house.

A person with a job who gently tries to get everyone to leave the house together.

A bratty little unformed person who practices raising her eyebrow as a hobby.

And a girl person who would just like everyone to leave her alone by the window while she is trying to take photos of a mysterious walker.

These people. They would make for an interesting story.

chapter 2

My strange story begins inside a story. I really did come into this world believing I was a character in a book. For this, I blame and thank my parents. That is odd, I know. You see, it takes about ten years for anything that's broken in our house to be fixed. I mean fixed-fixed. Completely fixed or replaced-fixed. Not *Oh, isn't this duct tape a creative way to keep the car's glove box closed?*

No, it's not creative. It's sort of dumb. And it's not really fixed, is it?

But that's how things work around our house. So when I was two and jumped up and down on my bed "with the ferociousness of a wild beast" (my dad's words), I broke the metal frame that held up the mattress. My parents "fixed" the bed by propping up the broken corner with a whole mess of novels and chunky art books. Ten years later, there is still a stack of books propping up my bed. And Mama comes in and takes one and replaces another like I'm a library. What is the result of sleeping on a broken bed frame propped up with books? All the stories and images have seeped into my dreaming brain. I think this is why I'm unusual and often narrate my own life.

Well, there are worse things a girl could do with her mind.

At first my narrations were just childish things.

Here is a girl about to take over the land of Bathrobia!

Mama and Dad clapped and told me I was so original.

And then I let my dreams take me places I wanted to go.

Here is a girl riding a red bike through the streets of Paris, France. (I have long believed I was meant to be a French girl.)

Mama and Dad said that I would make a very nice French girl.

And then I let my narration solve my problems.

Here is a girl whose mother is driving the entire family to a restaurant where they make giant pizzas.

Mama and Dad looked at each other and said nothing.

"Did you like my story?" I asked.

And Mama said, "You're not really in a story, Mysti."

"But I am. It's not just my dreams that are different. It's our whole life!"

"We are a little different," Mama said. "But we have a lot of love."

"We've never been to a restaurant."

"I know."

"Well, why not?"

And she said, "Go fold your clothes before they wrinkle. We'll talk about that some other day."

Some other day never came. I stopped narrating bits of life in front of my parents. I only liked it when they agreed that my stories were possible.

I don't know much, but I realized that we don't really fix things good and done in my family. We hold them together with tape—real or imagined—and pretend everything's peachy. It's a trick not unlike being quiet at school so that kids will think you are smart.

I've thought about it and realized that maybe going to a restaurant isn't a necessary life skill.

The fact that we never go to a restaurant just became the topic we didn't speak of.

The fact that I knew other kids whose mothers actually left their houses stopped seeming so exotic.

The fact that my mom was a stay-at-home mom, a literal *stay-at-home* mom, became just that. A fact. She stayed at home all the time and painted and gardened and made fresh bread every other day and, yes, created a lot of love. And I began to wonder if a person really needed a mother who drove a car. Maybe one parent with a driver's license is enough.

Laura, my little sister, and I went to and from school on the bus. Sometimes we'd get a ride home with a friend. With Dad, we'd go to get groceries or school shoes or sometimes to the park. Once in a while, there was a trip to a doctor for a checkup. Once a month, the three of us would go to the local library. Dad was always the one behind the wheel of the old green Toyota with the duct-taped glove compartment, and Laura and I were always the passengers. Never Mama.

And we'd come back from wherever we'd gone and find Mama waiting for us at the kitchen table, reading an art book right next to the set of black-and-white hugging salt and pepper shakers. They look like two little ghosts in an embrace, and they've always been smack in the middle of our table. For a long time, I thought Mama read to them while we were gone.

Okay, salt and pepper, let me read to you about how to create harmony with color.

Mama's stay-at-home-ness was spoken of between Mama and Dad only in the night hours when they thought no one was listening. (But who cannot hear things inside a tiny house with thin walls?) There were little arguments over pamphlets she didn't want to read. The pamphlets on the subject we're not supposed to talk about were stuffed inside her *Good Housekeeping* magazines hidden in her nightstand drawer. I discovered these secret documents two years ago. (The insides of drawers need to be dusted, too.) I read some of them. Okay, I read all of them. I came to understand that Mama had something called agoraphobia, which according to those pamphlets meant having a strong fear about being in places or situations from which escape might be difficult, be embarrassing, or cause panic attacks.

No amount of paint could cover the thin walls of our house enough for me not to hear their soft voices describing how Mama felt this kind of fear. (Or maybe I crept down the hall and put my ear to their door.)

"Maybe just go out the front door and take a walk."

"I don't know, David."

"Well, you don't need to leave right now; you can practice later. Just practice. Practice takes courage, I know, so just take small steps. It would be good, you know for the girls to see you try."

"It's not like I want to be this way," Mama said. "But I—"

I never heard the rest of her sentence.

But every time I dusted in Mama's room, I read the

pamphlets again. I wanted to make sure they were real. I never forgot this sentence: *A highly developed imagination is often found in children of agoraphobic parents.*

In the end, I considered that because I was a child of an agoraphobic parent, I'd come by my highly developed imagination naturally. It wasn't just those books propping up the broken corner of my old bed that made my mind stir with stories. It was also the benefit of having an über-stay-at-home parent. So I quit asking questions about other mothers and restaurants.

Dad quit trying to get her into the car to practice being courageous. Everything was fine. I guess as far as they were concerned, everything was fixed.

But if you keep turning the pages, the story will change. I'm not a huge fan of change. I don't like outgrowing my favorite shirt and having to look at my sister wearing it. I don't like daylight saving time, when all the clocks get out of whack and the light through the windows changes before I'm ready to wake up. I didn't even like it last week when the cable TV company decided in the middle of the night to change the channel lineup. Channel 130 is no longer Animal Planet but suddenly some stupid cooking channel.

"Why did they change this?"

"Change is good. Change teaches you to adjust," Dad

said when I complained about the TV. Dad is a good listener. He will look you right in the face and say that change is coming for all of us, that it's the way of the world so we should be prepared. When Dad says "Change is coming for you," it sounds like a warning. It sounds like a big, flat-footed monster creeping through the streets in the night. *It's coming for you!*

"Well, you want to go to Paris someday, right? You talk about it all the time," he said. "How are you going to get there if not by change?" There's no denying that I want to go to Paris. I want to *be* there. But I don't want to *go* there. All the travel and how to get there and the complications of it make me wish you could just be magically beamed where you want to go.

"You get to Paris by flying, Dad!"

"Well, let me know when you grow wings."

Dad. Always making a joke when I want him to be serious. That will never change.

chapter 3

Here is a girl with long red hair, age twelve and two minutes, who wonders why the house is so quiet.

Maybe they think I'm unprepared for their surprise. I'm not. I'm decidedly ready for it.

I step into the hallway.

The house is too quiet. No showers running. No Cheerios hitting the bowl. No TV news reports broadcasting strife in a distant city. Nothing. Even my dog, Larry, is silent as a log.

And then,

"She doesn't even know what's about to happen."

I hear the whispering. My little brown-haired sister, Laura, giggling. A conspiracy is afoot.

I know what they are trying to do. Do they think they can trick me? Me? In our tiny, tiny house that's so small you can hear a dust bunny poop?

This is probably all my dumb sister's idea. I grab a handful of marbles from my bookshelf and hop across the hall to her room. I pull up her bottom bedsheet and spread the marbles all over. Later, she'll think she's sleeping on rocks.

Here is a girl about to turn the tables on her unsuspecting family.

I get on my hands and knees and crawl toward the dining room/art studio. My dog, Larry, sidles up to me and almost gives away my cover.

Shoo, Larry.

Then, I peek into the kitchen. I spot them. Their backs are to me. All in a huddle of intended surprise. They don't even know what's coming. They are expecting me to walk by the kitchen table. But there are two doors to the kitchen and none of them is watching this door. That's a rookie move, not guarding both doors.

"Surprise!"

They spin around. Mama jumps and hollers and grabs the countertop. "Oh my gosh, Mysti!" She puts her hand to her heart.

"Gotcha!" I say, and then I fall over laughing.

But now they are all smiling and happy as the paint color Lemon Yellow. I have to take a moment to really see what my eyes see.

Wrapped presents. A tall chocolate cake with twelve candles. One for each year I haven't been anywhere else but here.

"Happy birthday, Mysti!" Dad says. "Twelve, huh? Make a wish!" Twelve years from now, I will be in France. That is my wish. *Poof*, the candles are out and my wish is a smoke signal to the universe.

Mama hugs me. Then she pulls out something from behind the bread box.

"Now, it's not completely dry yet." It's an oil painting. A really beautiful painting. Red poppies in a sea of yellow-green grass. A pale blue sky. A red-haired girl in white shorts with her hair trailing behind her. Carefree me in an unknown place. Maybe France. Definitely France.

"Thanks, Mama." The painted me has never looked so good. In real life, I wish I looked as good as this painting. The long red hair matches mine. The light blue eyes. The tiny freckles across my cheeks. All that is fine. What doesn't match is that the painted girl has a nice smile. The real me does not. The real me has a mile-wide gap between my two front teeth. The real me does not smile like this. Why would she?

Dad presents me with a red kite, a book of jokes, and an IOU to fix the zigzag crack in my ceiling.

"Why didn't you just give me a roll of duct tape so I can fix it myself?" I tease.

"Hardy-har, Mysti! Hey, why don't cats play poker in the jungle?"

"Why?"

"Too many cheetahs."

Like me, my dad has thick red hair and blue eyes and the love of a good joke.

"Open mine next," Laura says, and I do. A book of stories I'd begged for. There are lots of blanks and you get to fill in some of the story ideas and change the direction of the plot. According to the back cover, within the pages there are 267 story possibilities.

I've tried to get the little brown-haired brat to pretend she's in a story, too. *We could each write chapters*, I said. *We could invent magical lands or trips to the moon or being rock stars who sell Girl Scout cookies*, I said.

Here is a girl giving wonderful lyrics and a box of Thin Mints to the president.

And Laura always says, *No, tell me your stories, Mysti*.

Laura. She's less of a do-it-yourself girl and more of a do-it-for-me kind of person. (I don't think she was born with a highly developed imagination.)

So I tell her my stories. Her favorite is about an eaves-dropping owl.

The owl leans in near the bedroom windows of little girls. He listens. He gathers bits of talk about Barbies who lost their heads. And when he tells his friends what he heard, they just say, Who? Who?

And he has to gossip again.

Laura applauds. Laughs. And then kicks me out of her bed.

"I'm tired now. Go back to your own room," Laura says.

Well. Some listeners are ungrateful. Ungrateful listeners get marbles under their sheets.

"Eggy doodles for breakfast!" Mama announces. She spreads out a nice ironed tablecloth and sets up the kitchen table like we are in a fancy restaurant. Then she makes the most fabulous ham-and-cheesy eggy doodle in the history of eggy doodles.

"Eggy doodle for the birthday girl!" Mama says as she places a plate in front of me.

"And what about braces? This is the year for braces, right?"

There it is. The sharp glance between Mama and Dad. I know what I am doing, playing this trick. Even my dog,

Larry, knows I will not be getting braces this year. Because even Larry knows there is only one adult here who drives.

"We will discuss it," Dad says finally. "How about you tell us a joke from your book?"

"We will discuss it" means that it will probably not be discussed anytime soon. I pick up the joke book.

"Why won't aliens eat clowns?" I ask.

"Why?" says Dad.

"Because they taste funny." That's not a bad joke. After breakfast I will text that joke to Anibal Gomez. Anibal Gomez is my one friend. I'm not still and quiet in front of him. I am myself.

chapter 4

Here is a girl winning the Nobel Prize for inventing a mobile orthodontist business that drives down neighborhood streets, and all the kids with crooked teeth chase after it and receive straight smiles.

Anibal Gomez isn't bothered by girls with bad teeth and transportation issues. And I'm not bothered by shy boys who are size extra, extra large, which is what he is. Anibal has someone to sit with him on the bus, and I have someone who won't invite me to parties I will just have to say no to. (As they would say in France, this friendship is *parfait*, which is French for "perfect.")

I shared with Anibal this last story excerpt about winning the Nobel Prize for mobile orthodontia.

"You have crazy ideas," Anibal said. "Of all the mothers in the world, your mother is the least likely one to let you go chasing after a random orthodontist."

"It's a story!"

"I guess that *could* be a good idea for you," he said. "Especially since your mama—"

"Shut up!" I interrupted. "Don't say it."

"I was just going to say since your mama won't have to keep looking at your teeth. Geesh. You're so sensitive."

If you know Anibal like I do, you would know that is a compliment. Sort of. He didn't say the secret thing about Mama.

One day during fifth-grade recess, we traded family secrets.

"Since I was eight, I've had to sleep on a broken water bed filled with stuffed animals," he said. Of course, I loved that his family also fixed things in unusual ways.

"Since I was five, my mother has never left our house," I said. I waited. Nothing. Not even a blink. It sealed Anibal Gomez as my best friend.

"My mother works at the dollar store," he said. "I can get you a Justin Bieber poster."

"My mother grows cantaloupes in the backyard," I said. "And my dad eats them all, and I don't care for Justin Bieber."

Anibal is still the most trustworthy person I know.

There's no trying to discover his hidden meanings, which I have to say is a problem I have with girls. They are all "Guess what I'm thinking," and Anibal is all "Here's exactly what I'm thinking."

Which is why I took Anibal at his straightforward word when he called to wish me a happy birthday and to present a new idea. A theory, really.

As long as Anibal is in the world, there will never be a shortage of theories.

"I'm conducting a social experiment. You will be part of the experiment."

"What do I have to do?"

"Pretend you don't know me."

"Why?"

"I've decided to be a hipster this year."

"You can't just decide that. You have to be called that by someone first. Develop a reputation."

"I bought a hat," Anibal said. "And I think Sandy Showalter likes the hipsters. This is the year of Anibal and Sandy. Sandy will notice me and go with me to the fall social. She probably won't notice me if, you know, another girl is in the way. So, there you go. That's how you are part of the experiment."

"But why not just introduce yourself to Sandy? Even I could do that."

"It's the theory of the world, Mysti. Girls like Sandy

are only nice to people who fit in. The world is cruel that way, but what are you gonna do?"

"Are you saying I am a person who does not fit in?"

There is silence on the other end of the phone. Loud silence.

"I don't know," I finally said. "Why should I do this for you?"

"Two words. *Talent. Show.*"

"What? Wait a minute. I have to think about this," I told Anibal.

"Talent. Show!"

"Okay, I get it."

Lightning and thunder. I knew those two words would come back to haunt me one day.

chapter 5

Here is a talentless girl who had the impossible dream of winning the Beatty Middle School talent contest.

Last year's talent show was not one of my better ideas, I admit. Maybe it was a story idea that should've stayed in my head. I'm usually more cautious about putting myself in the white-hot spotlight of embarrassment. But when I picture myself with Anibal, well, everything else—the kids' comments, gum stuck on my shoe, a bad hair day—all those things fall away like dry leaves.

So I'd written my name down with Anibal, and he said he'd do it if I came up with the talent. We didn't know if we had any talent beyond surviving the bus ride home and making fun of our lunches.

You call that a tuna sandwich?

No, I call it Fred.

Who eats a hot dog without a bun?

Someone whose mother forgot to buy buns.

So I asked Mama what I should do for a talent.

"Oh, won't you be scared up on that stage? Is it high off the floor? Do you think you'll fall?"

I asked my dad.

"What? I don't know. Tell some jokes. I love that one about the cow."

I asked my sister, Laura.

"Too bad you can't sing like me. Taylor Swift better watch out!"

I went to get the mail and asked our next-door neighbor, Mrs. Jennings.

"Can you sew? I won a contest in high school by sewing my own pants. They were red!"

I carried the mail toward our brown front door and spotted the mysterious Woman Who Goes Somewhere across the street. *Hey, what kind of talent would you like to see performed by two eleven-year-olds?*

I chickened out and didn't talk to her because I suspect Woman Who Goes Somewhere is full-moon crazy.

I tallied up all the results of my survey on a piece of paper.

Tell a joke.
Sing.
Sew red pants.
Walk on by.
Just don't do it because it's scary.

I favored the last idea, which was Mama's.

But I did it anyway. It's true that Mama is pretty much afraid of everything. She has a belief that nefariousness is everywhere. And sometimes, I try to do the opposite to test out my own hypothesis of fear. (Because the main thing I'm afraid of is not getting to Paris.)

So your garden-variety talent show. What's to fear?

As it turns out, a talent show includes what we might call "unknown fears."

It was two days before the talent show and no talent was showing up. So I wrote a poem, which in my opinion had a lot of depth and angst for a person of my young years. It included the words *vast* and *formidable*. Its theme called up a person who rarely left the house.

She was a person who rarely left the house.
During the day, she was quiet as a mouse.

"We're going to embarrass ourselves," Anibal said.
"I know. It was a stupid idea."

"No, it was brave," he said, handing me a Mentos mint. Anibal Gomez is never without a mint and a word of encouragement. Fresh breath and support are good qualities in a friend.

We followed through. We were brave. Our names were called right after Kelly Springfield finished performing a baton-twirling routine that seemed to defy the rules of spine structure.

Principal Blakely announced, "And now, a performance by, um, Anibal Gomez and My-sty Murphy. Oh, sorry, that's Mist-ee Murphy."

This was no time to consider how I hated my name with a red-hot passion. We walked onto the stage and collected the last scraps of Kelly's applause, which was a good thing because that was the only real clapping we'd earn. Four hundred pairs of eyes watched us perform across the cafeteria. I was nervous. Someone—I think it was my mother—said you should picture the audience naked so that you don't get nervous while speaking in public. My advice? Don't do this. It will make you turn red and forget what you came to do.

Anibal rapped a beat while I read my poem.

Vast. Formidable. Mouse.

Boom dig a boom boom!

Anibal did a great job. He's got skills.

We soon learned what the sound of a slow, sarcastic clap sounded like.

Vast.

And then the shouts. *Hey, AniBALL! That performance was just like you. LARGE!*

No matter. We brushed it off like crumbs off a table. Gone. We came to do what we signed up for and had a great laugh on the bus. Other people had a great laugh on the bus, too, if you know what I mean.

For two days I thought about Anibal's request to be in a social experiment. This is a big change. A colossal change. And we know I'm not the president of the fan club for change.

Finally, I called him. "Okay, I'll go along with your I-wanna-be-a-hipster experiment. Not all your ideas have been this lame."

"We won a science fair ribbon, didn't we?" Anibal asked.

"Yes." We won last year for our lame deodorant-comparison experiment.

"And it's only during school hours, you know?" Anibal offered. "Besides, you'll enjoy the show. You will see me in the hallways and be in awe of my skills."

"I'll try to contain my amazement."

"Feel free to take pictures of my new and improved seventh-grade awesomeness and send them to my phone."

"Whatever," I said. "I have to go play Little House on the Prairie now."

"More cantaloupe?"

"Isn't it always?"

I hung up the phone and took stock of my situation. I'd be a seventh grader in a week and would have to temporarily pretend I didn't know Anibal Gomez during school hours so that he could prove his theory of social coolness. These are the kinds of things you only do in the name of friendship.

There are harder challenges in the big blue world anyway.

chapter 6

Here is a girl washing green beans, extracting melons, and contemplating the true meaning of friendship.

Blue-sky Saturday afternoon. The air is so still and hot and the sun is so blinding that a person could melt if she's not careful. I don't know how those vegetables stand it, especially the ones along the fence line that burn under the sun all day long. They must feel like they are on the death row of gardens. Of course, I know vegetables don't have feelings, but still. We make them bake all day and then we murder them for dinner.

I've finished giving the green beans a good soak and pull up about three ripe melons from the farm known as our yard and still can't shake off this empty feeling. Normally, I can make it vanish by doing all my chores, but not today. It's as if I've been let down gently. A cloud in the sky that God's hand just set down on earth and said, *Oh, please stand over here by yourself while I admire all the other clouds.*

The funny thing is, we haven't even started the stupid social experiment and I'm already missing Anibal Gomez. Because somehow the idea that I, Mysti Murphy, would get in the way of Sandy Showalter doesn't fit. Anyone with eyes knows I'm no competition, romantically speaking. And then there's just the idea of Sandy and Anibal together. Getting Sandy Showalter to notice him is not exactly an impossible dream. I mean, I could dye my hair purple and get someone to notice me. No, the real challenge to Anibal's experiment is that he thinks Sandy would consider going to the fall social with him. That is the part that makes me laugh every time I think about it. There are some girls who don't mix with guys like Anibal. Sandy is one of them. But maybe that was a sixth-grade rule. It's not as if I'm the author of the *Middle School Handbook on Social Skills*. Maybe in seventh grade, things change.

I get out my new English Red kite and lie down in Mama's garden next to the tomatoes. My free thinking time is over before it starts because Dad sprays me with the water hose.

"Gotcha!"

"Dad!"

"You're cooled off, aren't you?"

My dad. He's in the driveway washing the car, and lifted that green hose right over the fence just to soak me good. There is a piece of duct tape around the end of the hose that covers a leak.

"Going to the store with me later?" Dad shouts.

"Yeah."

"And maybe ice cream?"

"Definitely ice cream."

Here is a girl enjoying the bright sunlit rays of her parental unit's love.

"Now that you're twelve, you can drive, right?"

"Dad!"

Now, he lets fly one of his car-washing towels. It soars in the air until it gets plumb stuck in a high branch of the giant tree.

"Oh, will you look at that?" he says to the tree. "Be right back."

The giant tree.

It's ancient and big and Deep Ochre. Would it be fun to climb? Well, yes, depending on which parent is in our backyard.

If Dad wrote a book, it would be titled *Go Climb a Tree and See the View!*

If Mama wrote a book, it would be titled *Get Down from There Before You Hurt Yourself!*

The giant tree sits squarely between our house and the Jenningses', right in that raft of grass that separates our two driveways. It was probably planted by the first settlers to Texas.

While I wait for Dad to climb the tree, I climb the part of our backyard fence that faces the street, hoping to spot Woman Who Goes Somewhere and get another clue about her travels. Laura bounces outside and sidles up to me.

We peer through a cookie-sized hole in the wood fence. Sure enough, the mysterious Woman Who Goes Somewhere flip-flops past our house in sweatpants, a baggy emerald-green sweatshirt, and a yellow flower in her hair.

"I'd love to follow that woman to see where she goes," I say.

"What if she is nefarious? What if she snatches people and Mama has to make HAVE YOU SEEN ME? T-shirts?"

"Oh my gosh, Laura, don't get all worked up. The woman doesn't even have a car, so how could she do any real snatching? Geesh." The topic we don't speak of is *not* producing a highly developed imagination in Laura. It's producing a little seven-year-old Mama.

Now Laura says, "Well, I think I'd like to know what she does every day. It can't be good."

"She has a square object in her pocket that could either be an intergalactic remote control or a wallet," I say.

"It might have something to do with space or shopping."

"You're not as stupid as you look."

"Mysti!"

"Also, she doesn't care what she has on or even if her hair is brushed, so we know she is not going to a fashion runway."

I explain to Laura that it's possible the woman is walking toward a TV show for the surprise makeover of her life. Her stringy hair will be brushed to a golden sheen and a hair artist will put blond highlights all around her face. She will wear sparkly pink lip gloss and just a hint of mascara. She will be dressed in dark jeans, sandals, and a flowing shirt spun from silkworms in Egypt. Her new earrings will feature diamonds and rubies from Queen Elizabeth because the queen woke up that day and said, *Jewels for all the walkers of the world!* When the Woman's new makeover is revealed, she will walk onstage and smile a smile worthy of Miss America. Yes, she will be amazingly beautiful and the camera operators will faint. A TV director will shout, *Get up, you camera operators, and then ask the Woman why she never got a makeover before.* And the

Woman Who Goes Somewhere will reply that she'd been walking around the world, picking up rocks and flowers and bits of grasshopper legs that when mixed together in a soup create a natural and tasty cure for cancer, so who has time to apply mascara.

"You should write that down, Mysti," Laura says. "It's one of your better stories."

Laura is so easily entertained by stories, which is about the only quality in her I appreciate. But what I would love more than applause for my creativity is to really and truly unlock the mystery behind Woman Who Goes Somewhere. There are probably 267 possibilities. But do you know when I will be able to follow the Woman to find out where she goes? The twelfth of never.

"*Merci beaucoup,*" I say to Laura.

Here is a girl with storytelling that is admirable and colorful being awarded a giant unicorn, a new iPad, and a brilliant school wardrobe that would make people take back ridiculous requests for social experiments.

"Girls, oh my goodness, get down from there before you hurt yourself," Mama shouts, and we do as she says.

While I wait for Dad to take me to get ice cream, I brush my hair into a ponytail and then rearrange the posters on my corkboard and place Mama's painting on my nightstand. I flip through my new storybook and put it back on my shelf with all my favorite stories that are set in France (*The Invention of Hugo Cabret, Madeline, The Red Balloon, Madame Pamplemousse and Her Incredible Edibles*).

Now I smell the wonderful scent of fresh banana bread Mama is baking in the kitchen.

Larry plonks down in his space right next to my bed.

I sit by the window and wait.

Everything is nice. Everything is calm.

But you know what they say about calm. It always comes before the storm.

That's when I heard the *crackle, snap, boom*.

The tired old tree branch gave out when Dad climbed on it to retrieve his car-washing towel. It sent him crashing headfirst onto the wet pavement. By the time we got to him, he looked peaceful, like he'd just decided to lie down next to the car and take a nap. The scene didn't look as nefarious as it should have.

chapter 7

Here is a sad, sad girl watching an ambulance drive away in the bright August sun.

You'd think the giant tree branches would have at least given a whisper of danger. *Don't climb up here, Mr. Murphy. Stay where you are and let the wind remove the towel in its own good time.*

No, there was just the sound of our next-door neighbor Mr. Jennings, screaming to the wind, "Call nine-one-one!"

And then Mama, whose ears are trained to hear 9-1-1 in her sleep, came out of her painting trance, dropped her paintbrush on the wood floor, and rushed out the door. She saw it all, and when I tried to go sit next to Dad, she pushed me and Laura away.

"Stay in our yard," she commanded.

And then the ambulance. A huge neck brace. A muscled paramedic telling me to *get out of the way, honey.*

A hot cry rose up in my throat but it didn't come out. Laura held on to my arm and watched it all happen and cried like the mushy girl she is. And Mama, her face was drenched with tears and her hands shook a little as the ambulance pulled away from the curb. Laura and I eased Mama to the porch.

"Darlings, do you want a ride to the hospital? Anything?" Mrs. Jennings asked. She'd carried over cups and a pitcher of ice-cold sweet tea and poured it out for us.

Mrs. Jennings. She's the only person who didn't realize the answer would be no. Mama couldn't get into her car. Mama couldn't get into *any* car.

Lord knows she's tried it a few times, but just sitting in the passenger's seat gives Mama a panic attack. She shakes and sweats and says she feels like she's having a heart attack. Dad rushes over. *Breathe into this bag, Melly. You're all right. We'll try again another day.*

And Mama breathes into the bag, comes out of whatever mental closet she went into to hide, touches his cheek, and says, *What would I do without you?*

Me and Laura, we've watched the Mama Tries to Ride channel a few times. We are not fans.

Why does Dad keep forcing her? Laura asks me in private. *It's mean.*

And I always say, *I guess he wants her to go places.*

But this day, the day of the falling tree branch, was not going to be the day Mama tried to go places. Not without Dad. Not even to go and see Dad. Worst of all, we were all thinking that same question. I could feel the imaginary bubble cloud form over our three heads:

What *would* we do without Dad?

Because if there's one thing we all know about the topic we don't speak of, it's this: Dad does everything that requires outside-the-house activity.

From the paramedics and the scraps of conversation I heard, I knew at least this much. Dad's head hit the pavement with such powerful "concussive force" that it might take a while to "assess his injuries," and that "surgery to remove pressure from brain swelling" is a possibility. I don't know much, but I knew we were going to be doing without Dad for a while.

Mrs. Jennings left and we sat on the porch, all three of us, in the hot afternoon sun. Melting. Worrying. Mama still had a streak of Violet paint across her cheek. It had smudged with her tears, and I tried without success to wipe it away. My fingers came away purple and salty, and she looked like she was bruised. I asked, "How long do you think Dad will be in the hospital?"

"I don't know," Mama replied.

"Are you going to stop crying?" Laura asked.

"I don't know."

"Can we go to the hospital to see him?" I asked.

"I don't know."

At dinner, we all sat down at the kitchen table to eat taco salad. The longer we sat in silence, the more the stupid hugging salt and pepper shakers irritated me. They stood there like nothing had changed and I hated them for it, which is stupid because salt and pepper can't feel hate.

"It's pretty serious," Mama said. "What happened to your dad." You could see in her still-watery eyes that she didn't really want to talk about him.

"So what does this mean?"

"I'm not sure. They will know more after surgery."

"But Mama, you can't drive," Laura stated. I gave her the evil eye. Laura is still too immature for her own good.

Mama stabbed at her lettuce.

"I know that, Laura," she snapped.

I kicked Laura. "It's going to be okay, Mama."

"Eat your salad."

If it comes to it, we can find someone to take us to the hospital. Maybe the Jenningses.

"Eat your salad," Mama said again.

"I'm not hungry."

"Then pray for your father." Her nose was red. Her eyes were all glossy from the tears. Dad always tells jokes and it makes Mama smile.

I opened the joke book Dad gave me. "Did you know that time flies like an arrow, but fruit flies like a banana?"

It worked. She smiled. A big, beautiful, straight-teeth smile. I love it when she smiles. My mother has days when she can be really beautiful. Especially when she lets her worries take a nap.

"Oh, bananas! I almost forgot the bread!"

Mama went to the kitchen and cut two nice thick slices of her fresh-baked bread.

Mama's answer to a lot of things is a piece of home-made bread.

Two days later. Mama has pretty much napped around the clock. We learned that Dad is in critical condition.

He had surgery to remove pressure from his brain. His doctor is hopeful.

Well, now I am bone tired from worrying, so I think I'll stop. The fact that Dad might wake up next to an empty vinyl chair is depressing. I've seen movies. I know there's supposed to be a person sitting next to the injured patient when he wakes up.

"We'll go see him soon," Mama says.

In the afternoon, I climb onto her bed and curl up next to her. She strokes my long red hair in the way that I love.

"You have about four different colors in your hair, Mysti," she says. "Chinese Red. Copper. Naples Gold. Poppy."

"You've told me that forever."

"Well, it'll be true forever."

"It won't ever grow in gray like yours?" Mama's roots are showing. The roots are the color of a dusty squirrel. The rest of it is French Roast Brown, or so it says on the hair-color box.

"I hope it doesn't, sweetie."

Judge Judy, Mama's favorite show, pops up on her TV and we lie there together, watching Judy tell people when to talk, how to straighten up, and to dare not try coming into her court with a lie, which in her world means something is baloney.

Today, there is a lady who walks up to the defendant's stand wearing a shirt with part of her belly button showing.

I say, "Ooh, she's gonna get it from the judge."

"What was she thinking this morning when she scanned her closet? Oh, this shirt will impress the judge?" Mama laughs.

Sure enough, Judge Judy asks Girl with a Bad Shirt if she forgot she was coming to court today. The girl looks clueless. She probably forgets a lot of things.

"Don't worry. Mr. Jennings will drive us to the hospital," I say.

"Maybe."

Girl with a Bad Shirt ends up having to pay the plaintiff. Who didn't see that coming a wardrobe away?

When Mama is asleep, I cover her with a blanket and go in search of a snack. I eat the yummy banana bread leftovers.

It's obvious to a blind flea that we will really need to talk about the subject we don't talk about. We need to take that question outside and shake it out like a rug. Because I looked up information about brain injuries on the computer, and I know one thing for sure: That big flat-footed monster called Change is coming for us, and he doesn't deliver groceries.

chapter 8

Here is a girl preparing to enter seventh grade with a dented dad, no obvious friend, no new school shoes, and the horrific realization that she'd only shaved one leg.

The first day of school.

It doesn't feel like we are ready for the first day of anything.

Every morning for the past four days, Mama sits in her room and watches TV.

Every afternoon for the past four days, we get a little report from Dr. Randolph at the hospital about Dad's condition. He is stable and his vital signs are good.

Every night, we eat a garden salad and wish there were four plates to wash instead of three.

This time last year, my greatest concern was if I should bring a purse to middle school.

I miss having that problem this morning.

I have problems that include a limited supply of new school clothes. A backpack with holes in it. Sneakers that already have 102 miles on them. And, of course, one unshaved leg. This last problem is entirely my fault.

I look at the clock to see if there's time to race to the bathroom and make my legs match, hairwise. The clock says, *No, and you can't even slip on jeans, those capris will have to do.*

Stupid clock.

Before we leave for school, Mama does the kind of organizing where she's trying hard not to show she's upset. She wipes down countertops that are already clean and alphabetizes pantry products that just don't care.

Sniff. Sniff.

Wipe. Wipe.

Flour. Soup. Sugar.

Today, she has her dark hair pulled up in a Coral Orange scarf, and a smear of Revlon Rose lipstick on her mouth. She looks like a worried cheerleader. But I guess she's trying not to be so obviously depressed.

"What are you doing?"

"Well…" She pauses. "Taking inventory, actually. Seeing how we can stretch what we have."

"Want to hear the joke of the day?" This is me, trying not to worry about Mama being home alone.

"Oh, Mysti," she says, a little startled. "Yes, please tell me a joke."

"How do you make a tissue dance?"

"How?"

"Put a little boogie in it."

"I like that one."

"Thanks." I give her a big hug, and she gives me lunch and a reminder of the safety rules. Don't talk to nefarious strangers. Keep your eyes open. Stay in a group or with a safety buddy.

"There is safety in pairs."

Yes, I know. Stay in twos.

Same thing with Laura. I stand on the porch and hear all three brass locks *click*, *click*, *click*. And then her voice through the door: "Mysti, I can still see you. Go on, now. I'm going to paint today. I'll be just fine."

I try to be fine, too.

During the morning announcements, I hide my unshaved leg behind my smooth one and scan the room for a safety buddy. (Or what other seventh graders might call a friend.) Until Anibal returns from hipster land, it would be nice to cultivate another friendship. I didn't really reach out to any girls last year, owing to the fact that my friendship needs were satisfied. In retrospect, this was not a great strategy.

Among the sea of new kids, there are new clothes and not a pimple to be seen, all obliterated by fifty dollars and a 1-800 call to Proactiv. There are two girls I recognize, but they are so busy whispering they do not notice me. One of the girls is known for drawing a turtle next to her name. Last year, Anibal Gomez asked her outright, *Why do you always draw a turtle?*

With surprising volume, the girl yelled back, *It's a* tortoise, *not a turtle!*

Kids like to make fun of her now, but she is bulletproof about it. Why? Because she has a friend named Girl Who Likes Horses. For some reason, there is always a girl in school who likes horses. Even Laura agrees. It must be one of the universal laws in the book of education.

1. The cafeteria must smell vaguely like cold soup and sneakers.
2. At least once, students must receive a beat-up textbook that appears to have been dunked in mysterious liquid.
3. There must be *that* girl who likes horses.

Beatty Middle School's Girl Who Likes Horses owns a ton of horse T-shirts and carries around a thick *Encyclopedia of Horses*.

From where I sit, I do not see that these girls have an opening for a girl like me, mostly because I lack an animal obsession.

I hide behind my hair like it's a curtain, wondering where Anibal Gomez is at this moment. I can't help thinking about him. It's like he owns something of mine and I want it back.

I overhear Girl Who Likes Horses say, "Have you seen him? The hat?"

"Don't you think it looks so hipster?" Girl Who Draws Tortoises asks.

Can they be talking about Anibal? Is a hat such a significant fashion statement to talk about on day one of school? Maybe there's something to his experiment. Note to self: Locate cute hat.

Last year, I would have told him about Girl Who Likes Horses and Girl Who Draws Tortoises and he'd have drawn a picture of a tortoise with a horse head. Man, he is good at drawing. I attempt to create my own doodle of a hortoise, but it looks like a donkey with a stomach disorder.

Anibal would do better.

After math class, no one has even waved at me. It is a little lonely and my mind drifts to the Sad Dad channel.

By third period, I switch to the Wishing I Was at Home channel, but all that's playing there is *How to Enjoy Cantaloupe with Your Mother.*

The next bell rings. Time for lunch. I'm certain to see Anibal in the cafeteria. I had sent him a text and know that we both have the B lunch period.

And there he is.

Anibal with a hat.

Anibal the hipster.

Anibal who was more than a little round in the middle last year and is now less round. In fact, he is half of his former self. Anibal Gomez is now in the category of cute boys. Boy-band cute. Truth-or-dare, who-do-you-have-a-crush-on cute.

Not that I do.

But I do have to admit that he looks cool. And that his secret plan to be a Sandy Showalter Attractor might just work.

I'm so happy for him that my happiness makes me forget all about our agreed-upon pact. I go right up to him and smile without even thinking about my tragic lack of orthodontia. A big, open dork smile that shows my gap.

"Hey," I say. "Who do you have for Texas History?"

Anibal is with two other boys who glance at me like I'm leftover meat loaf. We are all waiting for *the* introduc-

tion. The introduction is key. It is code for *I know you.*
Silence is code for *Why are you talking to me?* Silence is
what a lot of popular kids do right before they are going to
cut you down.

I can hear the ticking of my watch. It mocks me.

Awk-ward.

Awk-ward.

Awk-ward.

So I decide to help him out.

"So, are you going by Ani this year?"

We discussed this once. He'd go by Ani. I'd go by
Myst. New and improved, we said. New names for a new
year, we said.

"Are you going by Missed-teeth this year?"

Missed-teeth?

Oh. *Missed. Teeth.*

There is a roar of laughter from the other two boys.
Of course, they have nice, straight teeth. Maybe our new
names were supposed to be a secret and I just embarrassed him. Maybe he's joking with me.

"I'll save you a seat," I say. And then I remember, I'm
not supposed to talk to him. Too late.

"What for?" Anibal replies.

They disappear into the lunch line. Which is what hipsters must do, I suppose.

Here is a girl standing stupefied, her brown lunch bag with heart-shaped PB and J a sad companion to her misery.

Time stops. Whole seconds pass before I realize I've been hurt. Rejected. I tell myself it's just an experiment. He told me not to talk to him. I knew that. I'm just being a girl. Overthinking. Swayed by the heavy half of my life at home. This is nothing. Just go sit down and let the experiment play out. Let Sandy Showalter notice that Anibal doesn't talk to or notice any other girl on the planet except her. She is it for him. The supreme girlfriend. Then she can instantly fall in love with him, update her Facebook status to "In a Relationship," and go to the social. Hypothesis confirmed. Done. The End.

Well, even I know that is a fairy tale.

I tell myself to just go sit down and wait for the potential miracle to happen. But I don't know where to sit. Where you sit on the first day of school is where you will sit for eternity, otherwise known as the rest of the school year. It's important to know where to sit. Who to sit with. Plus, I sort of hate the cafeteria. It's the scene of the awful talent-show debacle from last year. And it's clear I'm not the only one who remembers our lame performance.

Here comes Joe Busby, knocking into my shoulder.

Joe Busby who started the fake applause last year.

"There's the crazy poem girl," he says.

Man, I hate this cafeteria with a red-hot passion. But a person's got to eat.

Across the lunchroom, Anibal Gomez and his two new friends emerge from the lunch line with cheeseburgers and bad attitudes. One of them shoves a petite girl wearing a French Ultramarine Blue scarf. Like a frame is to a painting, the scarf is to her face. Girl with Scarf spills her milk. Boy Who Shoves shouts "Sand Girl" at her until Principal Blakely says, "Have a little respect, sir!"

I look at the boy's shirt. Boy with Tag Sticking Out.

I hope no one tells him all day. I hope he wears that tag like a dork flag.

I watch as Girl with Scarf's eyes sweep the cafeteria for a place to sit. This marks her as an obvious sixth grader. There's a whole mess of new sixth graders wandering around, trying not to look so new. Girl with Scarf is failing at this. At least we are united in our first-day distress.

Or what I'm going to call the Social Abyss.

Which I seem to have fallen into.

It is a long, deep well.

"Find a seat, please," Principal Blakely says as he walks past me.

I'm forced to find a seat at the loser tables, a lonely place where dreams of popularity go to die. The Loser Island is an area completely separate from the rows of lunch tables spread across the cafeteria. It's where guests and parents come to eat with students, but since guests and parents hardly ever show up, it's usually occupied by students with no place to sit.

Like me.

And a hot mess of science geeks like Wayne Kovok, the third-tallest guy in the seventh grade.

About Wayne. When I first met him in the fourth grade, he liked to tell everyone that his last name was a palindrome.

Did you know my name is a palindrome, a word that reads the same backward and forward?

Wayne Kovok has never started a sentence without "Did you know." People call him Boy with Palindrome Name or Palindrome Gnome or just Wayne Dorkvok. Kids are stupid that way, but Wayne sort of brought it on himself.

I'm not hungry anymore, but I open my lunch anyway. Inside, there's a tiny painted note from Mama.

Have Fun! It is painted in Hopeful Pink.

Girl with Scarf finally makes her way to the Island.

"That's a pretty scarf," I say, because I'm hoping I won't be the only girl on Loser Island, even if that means she's a lowly sixth grader.

In return for my compliment, do you know what I receive from Girl with Scarf? A scowl that would melt butter.

Two more boys sit down at the Island and put their

54

faces right into their books, too. That's what you do to survive at this table. No eye contact. All business. Let's just get our lunches eaten and get out of here alive.

Wayne Kovok takes a bite of his sandwich and says of my lunch, "Did you know that the largest peanut butter and jelly sandwich ever made was forty feet long and had one hundred fifty pounds of peanut butter?"

"No, I didn't know that, Wayne. Cool."

"Hey, what's that you're reading?" I ask Girl with Scarf, because I must at least look like I'm having fun when Anibal walks by.

No problem. Your insult didn't sting at all. Having fun over here on the Island!

"It's called a book," she snaps.

Well. Clearly she's not conducting interviews for a lasting friendship. If she were my little sister, she'd be sleeping on marbles tonight, that is certain.

I guess I'm staring out blankly at her because she quips, "I'm just going to eat my lunch and not talk. I'm here for the education."

"Yeah, because being nice is not a life skill you are going to need in the world," I say. Wayne Kovok looks at me and gives me a thumbs-up.

"I'm going to be a surgeon, so I don't need to be chatty," she says. "My patients will be anesthetized."

"Lucky for them."

Then I eat my lousy homegrown carrots in silence. Anibal Gomez and his new friends laugh so loud across the room, you just know they are having a great time. In a strange way, this annoys me even more. Those are supposed to be my laughs. My jokes. My new and improved seventh-grade year.

I'm stuck on the Loser Island.

And now this is where I'll have to sit all year. Because of my stupid name and because Anibal Gomez is pretending to be mean as thunder. I'll have to sit here and watch all the Beatty Middle School life going on around me. Life and people and cute clothes and laughter and girls who get shoved or just text like maniacs or have nice, driving parents bring them Subway sandwiches on the first day of school. Teachers trolling the aisles for misbehavior and litterers. A sea of kids who, with the exception of Loser Island, all appear to have someone to talk to and something to talk about. All that noise and distraction of the lunchroom didn't matter last year because I was part of a set. Mysti and Anibal. Not exactly a set of hugging salt and pepper shakers, but two friends who looked out for each other and laughed about tuna sandwiches. And now one part of my set is gone and I feel all exposed and naked. Like a turtle without a shell.

"Wayne?"

Wayne looks at me over the rims of his glasses.

"Can turtles live without their shells?"

"No, a turtle cannot exist without its shell because its spine is attached to the outer shell. Did you know that Russian turtles orbited the moon before any astronauts ever did?"

"No."

"It's true. In 1968—"

"Oh my gosh," Girl with Scarf interrupts. She rolls her eyes to high heaven, picks up her tray, and paddles away from Loser Island, the folds of her scarf practically flying in her wake. If I didn't dislike her, I would admire her.

Change is coming for you, Dad had said.

Change is going to kill me.

This is going to be a long year.

chapter 9

Here is a girl who wishes she'd hidden a piece of chocolate birthday cake.

After school.

I feed Larry and look for a snack.

Just a box of dry crackers. No milk. Two bananas on the verge of doom. Whatever else we have is probably in the deep freeze or highly pickled on the shelves in the garage or in the pantry and needs a lot of pots and pans to cook. No one wants a can of soup when they feel blue. You want something that's just right there in front of you, that you don't have to pick raw from the garden.

Which I could do.

Laura Ingalls probably did that in *Little House on the Prairie*.

Well, Dad and I were supposed to do our grocery shopping. The list is still taped to the fridge. I pull it down. It's just a reminder of what we don't have.

Milk
Dog food
Apples
Eggs
Bananas
Hair color (French Roast Brown)

And on and on.

Mama comes out of her room and makes a cup of tea. We ask each other questions about our days. Apparently, we were both "fine" all day.

"What about our food supply?" I ask.

"Really, Mysti, you make it sound as if we're trapped on an island," she says, ruffling my hair like, say, you might do to a dog. "Food supply, ha! Is that on your list of jokes?"

News flash: If an island is an isolated area from which you need some type of vehicle to depart, then yes, 4520 Fargo Drive qualifies as an island.

Mama slips off into her room so that she can wear her worried face behind closed doors.

Yeah, we are all fine.

The thing to do is to stop thinking about food, like a fresh, crunchy apple or an eggy doodle sandwich or a piece of chocolate cake. Stop thinking about anything out of my reach, like achieving the right look to gain popularity. Stop wishing for the magical powers to either heal injured fathers or transport myself to the empty vinyl chair in Dad's empty hospital room.

So far, seventh grade will not go down in the story of my life as a year to remember.

It is time to pretend I'm in a story far, far away. I picture myself diving into a story the same way a person dives into a swimming pool. Headfirst and quickly submerged. Today's story is one where I will be in Paris and go buy a buttery croissant anytime I choose. To get the story rolling, I go and gaze at that wonderful, glittery tower that is always there for me, night and day. In our home office, the Eiffel Tower cam is one click away on our computer. I swivel around in Dad's office chair and wait for the image to load. A stupid advertisement finally finishes and I am looking at a live view of the City of Lights. It's night in Paris and my beautiful tower is illuminated against a rich Indigo Blue sky. There is a light rain in Paris right now. Little droplets of water cover the camera lens that films the Eiffel Tower. I close my eyes and imagine what French rain might feel like on my face. Doing this in front of a computer screen is stupid, but it is my story so who cares.

Anibal Gomez would think I was a mushy girl if he knew how much I loved this picture of Paris. Do you know when I will tell him? The twelfth of never.

Bonne nuit, I say, which is French for "good night."

After, I go out on the hot front step and wait for mystery to walk by. Woman Who Goes Somewhere might appear at any minute. She's been walking later in the afternoons now, which is lucky for me. I sit for a long time. Girl Who Has Nothing to Do but Wait. Then I'm rewarded for my patience.

Here she comes, Woman Who Goes Somewhere, with long gray pants that don't look washed and yellow open-toe pumps. Her hair is all tied up in a messy bun. And it looks like she's carrying a small, round metal object in one of her hands. Quickly, I snap her picture as she is in full stride toward some adventurous destination. Today, there are not enough parents around for me to even get in trouble for infringing on other people's rights. So I take a picture of a car driving past, too. So what. Who's going to care?

I'm getting teary now. Mushy. I switch the channels on my brain.

I land on the Pick on Your Sister channel, one of my favorites.

Today's show: *Tricking Seven-Year-Olds into Eating Dog Food.*

Here we see the girl placing five bits of kibble in a shiny green bowl with the desired goal of sibling aggravation.

What I did was put about five pieces of Larry's kibble in one of Mama's pretty bowls and pretended I was chewing. Yum. Yum. Larry came running at the sound of snacks, but I had to shoo him away.

"It tastes like salty crackers," I told Laura while she was watching Animal Planet. "And also, Oprah says it will make your hair glossy and manageable."

"Will not."

"Fine, have dull, dry hair. See if I care."

Laura was convinced that I really did eat it because I already have one Oprah habit. I change my bedsheets every two days because I read that Oprah does this, too. Why can't I have at least one thing in common with a billionaire, you know?

If I see ten thousand faces in my life, I will never forget Laura's face when she began chewing. I chewed the inside of my mouth and tried not to laugh, but you know, I couldn't help it.

I am not a hateful person, but I do consider it my duty to play tricks on her. I've seen this in movies. I know.

After she swallowed that first dog food nugget, I laughed until I almost peed my pants. Seriously. Then I chased her through the house for the rest of the afternoon and told her she was going to wake up tomorrow barking. I only asked forgiveness after she went into her room and cried.

"Get out of here," Laura shouted.

"It was just a joke."

"You're horrible. You're a horrible, evil sister." She picked up a ratty old stuffed animal and threw it at my head.

"Didn't it take your mind off things? Aren't you tired of being cooped up in fourteen hundred square feet?" I threw myself onto her bed. Laura tried to push me out of her green room.

"Get out, Mysti."

"Well, don't you miss Dad?"

"Stop!"

"Wouldn't you want to be a dog for a day?"

"Get out!"

She said it so loud that I thought it might wake up Mama from her rest. I went into my room and changed my sheets like a billionaire. Clean-sheet day is the best.

I don't know why everyone doesn't do this. All it takes is soap and water and a small amount of effort. You want a little luxury, you make it for yourself.

When I'm done torturing Laura, my phone rings and sucks some of the luxury out of my night.

chapter 10

Here is a girl realizing that nefariousness travels across phone lines and crawls right into your ear.

"Hello?"

"I did good!" It's Anibal, wanting a report card for his horrible hipster performance.

"You can't be serious," I say. "You were awful. And I have a question."

"What?"

"How exactly is not being friendly with me helping you? Am I that horrid?"

I heard Girl Who Likes Horses use *horrid* in a sentence this morning, and it seems to be the new *gross*.

"No, I just need to be seen without any girls. I told you. It's an experiment. Nothing personal."

"I still don't get you."

"I think it's working. Sandy Showalter is in Texas History, dude!"

Anibal and I are in last-period Texas History together. Sandy and Wayne, too.

So Anibal strutted into class talking to Girl Who Plays in Orchestra, and they're all grinning like they visit Dr. Smile every week. Well, I couldn't help wanting to stare at him. That's how good and different he looks.

"You know what I think," I say to Anibal. "I think that hipster cap you bought is blocking blood flow to your brain."

"Your opinion."

"So cut it out."

"It'll work, trust me," Anibal says. "So don't talk to me tomorrow and I won't have to be, you know, a jerk. But that did help my reputation as a hipster, so . . ."

I don't say anything. There is a long pause until Anibal finally says, "Are you still there?"

"You don't even know about my dad."

"What?"

"You won't care anyway."

"What?"

"My dad's in the hospital."

"Are you kidding around?"

"No, I'm not!"

"Sorry, then. What happened?"

"He fell from this tree and smashed his head."

"Oh, man. I always thought your dad was cool. He let us smell his armpits for our science project. My dad wouldn't go for it."

"My dad is *still* cool. Don't talk about him like he's not around!"

"Geez, sorry. So, take my picture tomorrow so I can see what I look like in my hat." Anibal is not sorry.

"I don't like this at all."

"All experiments have their variables and controls, Mysti. You are the variable. You'll see that I'm right and will win."

"With Sandy Showalter as your prize?"

"If you want to look at it that way, yes."

"Sandy is cool and all and you are cool, but you're cool on different planets. Sandy is not really in your gravitational pull, with or without your hat."

"Says you."

"Anibal, face it, all the guys like Sandy. I mean, I have more of a chance of going to the social with her than you do." The words come out without time for me to think what I'm saying. I'd issued a challenge. Anibal Gomez loves a challenge.

"Are you betting me?" Anibal quizzes, proving how right I am.

"Well, not exactly." My brain is all confused. I don't know how fast I can backpedal and undo this.

"Betting me that you can visit Sandy's planet before I can?"

"This is redonk."

"So you can't?"

"No, I mean, yes."

"Then what? Take the bet! It will make this experiment so much more fun for me."

"Okay, I will take the bet only because it's not going to happen and at the fall social, we'll all be pretty much in our own orbits like always." I say this hoping that it will calm Anibal down and he'll see how tragically unrealistic it is to aim for the affections of Sandy. I hope.

It doesn't work. Anibal goes on about the terms of our bet. The official win would be proof of an actual text to and from Sandy.

"The text has to show some kind of flattery or compliment," Anibal says.

Anibal hangs up. I roll over on my side and look at *Faux-na Lisa*. Right now, her smile annoys me. Her constant happiness. Her always being on my wall, watching my every move.

How are you today, Lisa?
Oh, I'm fine, like always.

I get out of bed, take an old Eiffel Tower poster from my bulletin board, and tack it over the painting. *Faux-na Lisa* can look through the tower all night. I don't want to look at anyone, not even her faux French face. I close my eyes and let all the stories float up from the corner of my broken bed frame and into my dreams. I invite all of them in. Impressionist painters from a giant art book. Two of the Brontë sisters. Wizards from Hogwarts. Hemingway, who I haven't read yet, but is still invited to the party because he's Dad's favorite. I beg the authors, characters, and words to dance around my mind and make some kind of noise that will drown out the first awful day of school. But they say, *We're trying to come in, Girl Who Sleeps on Books, but there is no room here. All of your brain is currently being occupied by thoughts of someone named Sandy Showalter. We'll come back later when there's somewhere to sit.*

chapter 11

Here is a girl who doesn't even know Sandy Showalter, yet finds the girl staggeringly irritating for being the object of Mr. Gomez's affection.

Sandy Showalter.

She has the kind of first name you can actually find on pencils and key chains. There are no pencils with *Mysti* on them. I have looked. But there is *Sandy* on everything.

Sandy is part of the cheer squad at Beatty Middle School. Her perfect smooth hair is true and natural French Roast Brown. She could be the model on the box of Mama's hair color, in fact. And she smiles. Always smiles. The cheer squad walk around school all flatironed and together like a pack of unopened gum, all in perfect blue-and-white wrappers. They've all been to Dr. Smile, and so they smile, even with the sparkly braces showing. They are obsessed with the colors Cobalt Blue and Snowflake White, the colors of Beatty Middle School. On game days, the cheer squad wears cute blue shirts. They wear their hair in neat ponytails with a mess of blue-and-white streamers hanging down. They carry small dry-erase boards through the school with commands to *Go, Team* and *Get Fired Up* in blue marker. And I don't know for sure, but I think they have a rule that each cheerleader must bounce down the hallways, because that's what they do. You get hypnotized by the swaying ribbons. Ribbons of shiny blue and white against shampoo-model hair.

The cheer squad does not worry about falling trees and how they can change your life by making you count cans of dog food. They do not worry if they are in the hipster club. They do not worry about where they are going to sit at lunch. Wherever they choose to sit is automatically cool.

It would be obvious even to my dog, Larry, that I, Mysti Murphy, am not like the cheer squad girls.

It's not so much that I couldn't be one of them. You only need your parents' permission and a check for four hundred dollars. (And probably a good flatiron, which I do not have.) Even Girl Who Likes Horses is one of them. No, Mysti Murphy would not be on the cheer squad

71

because it involves a lot of transportation. Transportation is also something cheer squad girls don't worry about. They have mothers who take them to get frozen yogurt after school. They are the frozen-yogurt-after-school kind of girls. Pretty, frozen-yogurt-eating, blue-and-white-ribbon-wearing, flatiron-owning, Anibal Gomez–attracting girls.

"What're you looking at, Wayne?" I asked at lunch.

He put his head down. His cheeks went pink. "Nothing."

Those ribbons.

They must have special powers because that's the shortest sentence I'd ever heard Wayne Kovok utter in my life.

Sandy Showalter is not known to be mean. I even heard a fellow cheer buddy say, "Oh, your password is probably 'Be Nice,'" and they all giggled. But Sandy would sooner notice a dead cricket in a hallway corner than me.

Why do I get myself into these stinky pickles? Signing up for talent shows. Agreeing to social experiments. Throwing down the "I can be Sandy Showalter's friend" gauntlet, which will happen on the twelfth of never. Still, I take small comfort in the fact that Russian turtles orbited the moon before real astronauts, thank you,

Wayne Kovok. If a reptile can get in a moon's orbit, maybe a gap-toothed girl can get in the orbit of a popular, pretty, ribbon-wearing girl named Sandy. And if Anibal wins, then I will get him back as my friend. I guess it's now possible that I win either way, which makes me an undercover genius.

chapter 12

Here is a girl trying on the three hats owned by the poor, tragic Murphy family and, failing to achieve any kind of style, deciding against hat wear and opting for a barrette.

"Did you know that falling coconuts kill more people than sharks each year?" Wayne asks.

"What?" I say to Wayne.

"It's true," Wayne says. "Way more."

Lunch.

A few days into the school year and we have already formed a routine on Loser Island. We eat quickly. The gamers hardly look up, just reaching out blindly toward potato chip bags. Wayne Kovok shares a factoid. Girl with Scarf scowls. And I hide a cafeteria-made chicken-on-a-bun in my book bag for Larry to eat later, then munch on carrots.

Crunch, crunch.

Trivia.

Grimace.

Conceal.

Also, there is always the Anibal Gomez Trying to Be Cool channel for my viewing pleasure.

Today, Anibal watches Sandy Showalter and her magic ribbons as she and other cheer squad members bounce across the cafeteria holding spirit signs, smiling like it's the latest fashion accessory. You can just see little pink hearts float off Anibal's stupid hat. I feel a tiny bit sorry for him. To Sandy, he is also a cricket in the corner.

Sandy and her friends sit down at a great piece of lunchroom real estate, the tables near the stage. She applies clear lip gloss and sips juice through a straw. She makes middle school look easy.

"What are you looking at?" Girl with Scarf asks.

"Nothing."

"May I ask you a question?"

I brace myself for whatever stinging remark she's going to make about my carrots.

"Ask away."

"Um, should I carry a purse in middle school?"

Girl with Scarf is like the dollar-store candy machine. You put in your money, turn the knob, and wonder what is going to come out.

"No, no, you don't really need a purse. A book bag is fine."

"Okay."

"May I ask *you* a question?"

"Yes."

"Do you have a name or should we just refer to you as Dr. Grumpy?"

Wayne Kovok gives me a thumbs-up.

"Rama Khan," she says. "My name is Rama Khan."

"Rama Khan?"

"Yes."

She has great parents, this Rama Khan girl. Her name sounds like an action hero or a wizardly command. I write it down in my notebook when she's not looking. *RamaKhan!*

But by the time we get to Texas History, I'm still shaking off a compliment about Anibal I overheard in the hallways.

Oh, he's so cute in science! He kept untying my shoes!

I don't know much about much, but I do know

that if you're easily impressed by unlaced footwear, you are probably not going to grow up and change the world.

I'm not proud of this, but Anibal's growing reputation irritates me so much that I create a not-so-fabulous artistic doodle in my notebook while our teacher gets all animated about the state of Texas, as if we've all just gotten off a bus in the Lone Star State this very minute and need a tour guide with boots. Ms. Overstreet. She is not your typical twin-set-sweater-wearing breed of educator. I can tell that already. Her bluebonnet shirt is as bright as a blue-sky day. Her ability to spit forth facts is stupefying.

Sure enough, Wayne Kovok leans in and laps up Ms. Overstreet's trivia like Larry laps up water on a hot day.

"Texas is the only state to have had flags of six different nations fly over it. More wool comes from this state than any other in the nation. The Alamo is our cradle of liberty…and the name Texas comes from the Caddo people's word *teysha*, which means 'Hello, friend.' That is a great way for all of us to begin this school year. Let's all say *teysha* to our friends."

Blah. Blah. Blah.

No *teysha* for Mysti.

"Did you know that *Alamo* is Spanish for 'cotton-wood'?" Wayne asks.

"Very good, Mr. Kovok. I see you, too, are a fan of Texas freedom. *Teysha!*"

I wish a coconut would drop on my head right now.

Ms. Overstreet finishes her speech about how the history of Texas is of vital importance to all current and future Texans. That the legacy the heroes left us is to be revered and carried forward. That learning about the past is important to predict the future.

"So, cowgirls and cowboys, how can you know where you are going if you don't know your past?" Ms. Overstreet exclaims.

I write down *The History of Anibal*.

This may just be a social experiment. This may just be my way of insulting him in private. Maybe.

I continue drawing a stick figure of large Anibal of the past in my notebook. Then small, present-day Anibal. I thump cartoon Anibal with my fingers and imagine myself cutting him down in front of his new friends. I write that he is a stupid and formerly round you-know-what and uses discount deodorant that does *not* work.

Here is a girl with astonishing grace and finesse, informing the crowd that Anibal sleeps on a mattress made of stuffed animals.

"Miss Murphy, do you have something to share with the class?" Ms. Overstreet asks.

Ms. Overstreet holds a Texas-shaped coffee mug, which temporarily dazzles me because she is somehow drinking from the Panhandle. I've lived here all my life and can never get over how many different things can be made from the shape of Texas.

I shake my head "no," and my face and neck go red like Mama's tomatoes.

Right at this moment I really believe down to my bones that I am a character in a book, not just wishing for it to be true.

Do you know why?

Because what happens next has so much manufactured injustice it reeks of fiction.

Reeks!

Ms. Overstreet approaches my desk, spins my notebook, and inspects it. Her face contorts in a manner no wrinkle cream will ever undo. Next thing I am out in the hallway, waiting for the counselor, Ms. Peet, to come give me the "zero tolerance against bullying" speech.

Me.

Mysti Murphy.

I'm the bully.

Wait, I'm the bully?

How can that be? I just drew a meaningless cartoon, not a poster splattered across the Internet. When did quietly mocking someone in your notebook become bullying? Meanness, maybe. Lameness, probably. But if a true bully walked up to me right now, he'd tell Ms. Peet I was a pure amateur.

Ms. Peet has a soft, even voice and scolds me in the longest run-on sentence in the universe.

"I know this might seem like harmless doodles, but it might plant a seed of intolerance and you must show Mr. Gomez respect and not judge him and not ridicule his appearance, do you understand what I'm saying, Miss Murphy, really, we cannot have unfriendly doodles, sorry to be harsh with you, but we do expect the upper grades here at Beatty Middle School to set the example for incoming sixth graders."

When she says "incoming sixth graders," I envision actual sixth graders flying through the air like missiles, the teachers shouting *Incoming!*

Then I have to sign a form from Ms. Peet stating I will study the Beatty Middle School Rules of Tolerance and Kindness and commit myself to "being a buddy, not a bully," like all the signs plastered on the walls of the school say, but which apparently don't apply to nefarious individuals in the cafeteria who make fun of a person's unfortunate dental situation.

When the final bell mercifully rings, I run to my locker and pack up in a furious speed that could win me a berth on the Olympic sprinting-out-of-school team.

If such a team exists.

chapter 13

Here is a girl texting Anibal Gomez simply because she can.

Hey!

My plan is really working. Plus U got busted. So cool.

U R street rat crazy!

What about your dad?

Still sick

Sorry

Whatever

I mean it!

Thanks.

Do you need a stuffed animal?

Yeah, Big Bird's beak is keeping me awake.

Ouch! Call me!

My phone rings and for half an hour I talk about stupid things with Anibal. Really stupid things like posters and school projects and what's on sale at the dollar store. And then I pretend to want to know more about hipsters and listen to him talk about mustaches and specific grooming and his quest to find the perfect ironic T-shirt because he read an online article ("9 Ways to Be a Hipster") and it recommended this kind of shirt.

I grow bored of all this talk of hipster accessories and appearance and his Sandy infatuation, but I let it go. I just want to hear his voice. The truth is, I like knowing his voice is traveling right into the space of my ear across an unseen phone line, creating an unseen bridge of friendship.

chapter 14

Here is a girl with a mind full of worry and a stomach full of carrots.

September is here.

Unfortunately, nobody told the new month she could cool down a bit, summer is officially over. It's blazing hot and the house only has noise because the AC is still working at full tilt. Life without Dad shows us that he was the really noisy one in our family, because these days our house is mostly quiet except for the sound of my suggestions. Don't think I haven't suggested that we buy food online and have it delivered to our front door. We don't live under a rock or in a technological wasteland. We have an address and a computer.

"Well, Mysti, I don't trust food that someone else has handled," Mama said after I raised this idea. "Plus, the news says that nefarious people steal credit card information, and our garden will—"

Mama continued talking, but I tuned her out. She can let the air out of my idea balloons faster than you can say Larry.

Larry.

Larry's stomach is gurgling now because he's on a reduced diet. I'm cutting back a little until Dad can go to the store again.

"It won't be permanent, Larry," I tell him. He looks at me with big brown eyes. I love this dog. I love him too much to say that there are no new signs of progress about Dad. That I don't really know when I can give him a full bowl of kibble.

All I know is that Dr. Randolph predicts Dad will be better by Halloween. Eight weeks. Mama is marking off the days on the kitchen calendar with red pen and signing papers from an insurance company so that money can still come to 4520 Fargo Drive. And I work out how I can feed my dog, because the insurance company did not send dog food. These are truly the problems of the great story I'm living in.

"I can only give you half as much right now, boy," I told Larry.

Laura often ends up sleeping in Mama's bed now. Mama sleeps in a lot more days than she wakes. It's actually a blessing. She is easier to take care of when her head is on the pillow. When she's awake, it's like walking on eggshells. You say the wrong thing. *Crack.* The tears come. She tries not to cry in front of me when she is heating up a can of soup for dinner. I know she cries when she's alone. Her eyes are red when we come home from school, and she says it's because she just talked to her sister. I'm left to figure out what that means, I guess, but since her sister always pokes on Mama about the subject we don't speak of, I suppose that makes her cry. And it makes me mad at my aunt for being a jerk.

Today is a sleeping-in day.

So it's left to me to magically prepare a lunch for Laura and make sure she has her homework. I set up the coffeepot but use yesterday's coffee grounds and sprinkle a few new ones over the top, like Mama told me.

It will stretch our supply until Dad comes back, she had said.

We are all stretching.

Or shrinking. Larry is shrinking.

So I count the weeks until Halloween.

I count the number of frozen mystery meats way back in the deep freeze. Thirteen.

I count the remaining rolls of toilet paper in the hall closet. Ten.

I count the cans of dog food in the garage. Seventeen.

I count the scoops of laundry soap that produce clean-sheet day. (The unopened box says forty-four loads.)

I count.

I count.

I hope today she does not paint more ships. When she is sad, she paints ships or water scenes. I don't know why. That is between Mama and her paintbrush.

Now, it's not even eight in the morning and there is a storm of thinking in my head.

I think.

I think.

I think until my head hurts.

In math class.

"Did you see him today?"

I'm forced to hear Girl Who Draws Tortoises and Girl Who Likes Horses and all their sentences framed as questions. They continue to gush about Anibal. If only he liked one of them, half of my life problems would be solved. Maybe I should collect these compliments and pass them on.

"Isn't he *so* cute?"

"I know, right?"

"I wonder what kind of name Anibal is? Egyptian?"

"Do you think so?"

"He's changed so much from last year when he did that stupid talent show thing with what's-her-name. The girl who read the poem?"

Ahem.

They turn to me. I wave. "The name is Mysti. And I *wrote* that poem."

"Oh, well—"

"Why *do* you draw turtles all the time?"

"It's a tortoise!"

"Sure it is."

I thump my stick-figure drawing again. I should just stay quiet, like always.

Lunch.

Anibal and his friends get up and walk to the trash can. Anibal carries a book, and its title is turned out. Displayed for all to see. *The Catcher in the Rye*. Reading classic books was also on the list of hipster to-dos. There are so many items he's checking off that stupid list. Just yesterday, he finally wore an ironic T-shirt. It read FIGHT APATHY, OR DON'T.

This shirt made Rama laugh. But all this attention to

detail hasn't attracted the right girl. The one with blue-and-white ribbons and a key-chain name.

Still, my hope of talking to him bubbles up a little as he nears our table.

I sit up straight.

Smile.

Prepare.

Be ironic.

Here is a girl who believes her cheerful attitude might remind her friend of what he's missing.

"Trust the government," I say. I hold up my fingers in a peace sign.

"You get those shoes at Goodwill?" Anibal Gomez says, spreading around his mockery and misery.

"Funny. See you later, Anibal," I say nervously.

I stuff all my trash in my lunch bag. I don't even eat my cookie, which is something, since there was only one left and I could have given it to Laura. I should have given it to Laura.

"Did you know Goodwill began in Boston, Massachusetts, about one hundred years ago?" Wayne adds.

"No, thanks for that fact, dork." This is Anibal again. An equal-opportunity teaser.

"Do you know that guy?" Rama asks as Anibal struts away.

"Yeah, he's my best friend."

"Um, not from what I can see."

"Well, you can't see *everything*, can you?" I say sharply.

When I see Rama's face get all annoyed, I say, "It's a long story."

"I like stories," Rama responds.

"You wouldn't understand this one."

"Maybe I would."

That Rama. She gets to the point in a hot second.

Here is a girl wondering if she can trust a lowly sixth grader.

Rama follows me into the girls' restroom. The one by the library, because the one by the cafeteria is the mean girls' restroom and should be avoided at all costs.

"Why can't we go in there?" Rama wants to know.

"You go in and come out with something new to worry about. A girl says, *Oh, your outfit matches* really *well*, and you spend the rest of your day wondering if her tone conveyed sincerity or sarcasm, and by the time you go to bed, you realize that, yes, she was making fun of you."

"Got it. Not going into that bathroom ever," Rama says. "But about Anibal."

"Anibal has been my friend since the fourth grade. He's just joking around. Don't take it so seriously. Don't you have friends who joke around like that?"

"I don't have time for a lot of friends."

I want to say I'm shocked, but I just say, "Oh."

"It's not that I couldn't have a million friends, Mysti."

"I know."

"After school there is always practice, which is important. Violin practice and math practice and karate practice. I could have a lot of friends."

"You already said that."

"I don't like Anibal. Just the ironic T-shirt, that's all."

"He's not really like this. Remember how you were at first?"

"What? How was I at first?"

"Sort of like a porcupine."

"Well, I'm new here."

"So we all have our reasons for how we act. Same with Anibal. He is really nice. And smart. Way smart."

"People change," she says. Yes, yes, I could tell Rama. Change is coming for us all. I've seen its footprint all over our house.

Rama looks in the mirror and adjusts her scarf. "Besides, who needs him when you have me?"

"I didn't know I *had* you."

"Lucky you, huh?" Her smile is so pretty and soft, framed by a pretty scarf the color of Realistic Rose. But roses have thorns, too.

Rama leaves for class. I stay behind and steal a roll of toilet paper.

Then I get out the supplies to put the first step of my Sandy Showalter plan into action.

Texas History.

In the hallway, I time it just right and toss out my own tube of clear lip gloss at the right moment. Sandy will think she dropped it. Because Anibal is not the only seventh grader with a theory. I have theories, too. For instance, a girl like Sandy will notice lip gloss before she notices a paperback classic.

"Oh, Sandy?" I ask as I pick up the lip gloss.

Sandy turns to look at me. I hold up the lip gloss.

"I think you dropped this."

"Thanks so much!" Sandy beams and accepts the lip gloss. We're having this magical exchange right as Mr. Hipster breezes past in a cloud of Axe deodorant. Anibal looks at me sideways because he knows I made contact.

Here is a girl who fears that classic paperback novel will likely find a new home in a trash can.

chapter 15

Here is a girl traveling in the back of the longest brown car in the history of cars.

It's a hot Saturday in a supercool car—and by cool, I don't mean fashionable. I mean freezing.

But it was settled. Finally settled. The Jenningses could drive us to the hospital. After nagging and whining and *Yes, it's okay to ask neighbors for help, they said they wouldn't mind, now can we please, please go?*

Mama finds it hard to accept help from others. From anyone except Dad.

I don't.

Not for this, anyway.

It took little notes shoved under her bedroom door

and the tears of a mushy seven-year-old to get her to go along with this. But she finally said yes. I don't know why it was so hard. The Jenningses are anything but nefarious.

"Let's watch TV together when we get back," I told her as I left. "I'll change all the sheets, too."

I'm not certain that my words helped. Mama just nodded and locked the brown front door behind me.

When we finally get to the hospital, we meet with Dr. Randolph in person. He wears a white coat and has a twisty mustache. He looks like he knows a thing or three.

We are told Dad will have tubes and wires. We are told it might be scary. We are told to whisper encouragement into his ear.

Once Dad told me, *You will always be my lucky penny, Mysti.*

I take a deep breath and prepare to whisper into his ear. I could answer all the questions I know he would have if he was awake. I could say, *Don't worry. Mama is doing better than you would expect. No, she's not crying. She found a five-pound bag of rice in the cabinet. The turnips are coming in. School is fine. We are fine. We're all fine. So don't worry. I've got this covered.*

But I don't say any of that. I just say, "I love you."

He looks smaller.

His hair has been shaved like a military man.

There are tubes.

And the stupid empty vinyl chair I was worried about. If no one is going to be here, they should just take that thing out of his room.

Dr. Randolph puts his hands deep in his white coat and reassures us that he's "optimistic" about Dad's recovery.

Dr. Randolph says, "Next time, when your mother comes, your father won't have this tube here."

He says something else about muscle strength, but for me, his sentence came to a halt when he said "when your mother comes." *Hey, Mama, I know you are afraid to go out, but think about it, a hospital is really the perfect place to be afraid and panicky.*

I leave a stuffed bear in the empty vinyl chair. Oddly, it makes the chair seem more empty so I just tuck it under Dad's arm. Laura says it looks dumb and I want to pinch her. It takes all of my willpower to stay nice.

"You two okay back there?" Mr. Jennings wants to know as we cruise back toward Fargo Drive.

"Fine." *No, I'm not.*

It may be September outside, but it's downright January inside this brown car.

"Mysti, I wanted to tell you, I'm hatching a big plan," Mr. Jennings says. "An invention!"

Laura rubs her bare shoulders. I thank God for the invention of sleeves and that I thought to wear some today.

"What are you talking about?" Mrs. Jennings asks. "Hatching what?"

"The invention I told you about. The one for mixing ingredients."

Then Mrs. Jennings slaps him on the back and says, "Like all your other plans, Mr. Edison?" and he coughs hard and his false teeth come loose and he has to catch them with his hand before they hit the steering wheel.

"Mysti, Mr. Jennings has been dreaming up inventions since the day I met him but hasn't produced a single one," Mrs. Jennings says. "Nobody wants a sun visor with a clock."

"Ooh, I would," Laura pipes up.

"Mrs. Jennings forgets that *some* people might fall asleep in the sun and need an alarm," he says.

"Sure they do, sweetheart," she says. I think her statement is faux.

"Mrs. Jennings here seems to have forgotten how many attempts it took for Mr. Edison to invent the lightbulb. It took more than ten thousand tries. Dear girl, you *have* to read the Steve Jobs biography!"

"She's not going to read that doorstopper of a book!" Mrs. Jennings says. "She's too young, and that wouldn't interest her anyway. Mysti, I have some great books you can borrow. Maybe you'd like *Anne of Green Gables*?"

"Doorstoppers are the best kinds of books! And one is never too young or too old to be inspired by greatness!"

"I guess you were pretty inspired to marry me!"

"Marrying this old gal was the best decision I ever made," he says. His statement doesn't seem very faux at all.

This is how it goes. Back and forth. Inventions and sweet talk and book suggestions all the way home. I like it. It makes me wonder how many conversations Mama and Dad might have had while driving. Maybe they were sort of like this before their story included two daughters, a dog, and a house full of paintings. Mama had to go out sometime in her life. I've seen my parents' wedding photos. They sure didn't get married at 4520 Fargo Drive.

It's hard to picture Mama in a car, looking over her shoulder into the backseat, smiling at two daughters. I dig deep into my imagination and try to see her there. Woman Who Rides on the Passenger Side. Woman Who Has Conversations in Cars.

chapter 16

Here is a girl who has actually read The Catcher in the Rye
because it was recommended by her father.

Ur lip gloss trick was so obvious

Can you really name the main character in CITR?

Holden Caulfield! Boosh!

It's on the back cover.

So

So

Dad status?

Same. Dr. optimistic

That's his doc's name?

No, dweeb, his doc IS optimistic

Oh

L8tr

Wait!

Whut?

Need help w English

Topic?

Write acrostic poem about ur summer. Acrostic?

Pick word. Use as acronym that means something.

Such as?

S-A-N-D-Y. She attracts nerds daily, yo!

lol

chapter 17

Here is a girl annoyed by a fat, well-fed, non-store-shopping tree rat chowing down near the backyard fence of her childhood home.

Stupid squirrel.

Stupid tree.

Stupid lack of snacks.

When you go four weeks without grocery shopping, you realize how much you took the store for granted. Oh yes. When you can replace what you like to eat, life is simple. Your refrigerator is a place you can move things around in and search and think, *Oh yeah, I love baloney. Let's make an eggy doodle sandwich.* But then the fridge gets a lot of room in it and suddenly you can open it and scan with your eyes, no hands needed, and think, *Oh, since eggs are really important in an eggy doodle sandwich, I think I'll pass.*

And also, when you look at the back of the pantry and you check an expiration date on a dusty jar of red peppers and olives and wonder if it's still good, you think of stores in a new way. Then when your mama mixes the contents of that old jar with some rice for Sunday dinner and makes the "You better not say a word" face, you eat it.

And your sister complains, "This is gross. I'm not eating it."

And so you give her the double evil eye and a kick under the table.

Then you go to bed and keep your stomach superstill and pray to God that expiration dates are more of a suggestion than a rule.

That's what you have to do when you haven't gone to the store in a month.

In the afternoon, I search the kitchen, hoping I might discover something I'd overlooked.

"We're out of crackers," I shout.

"I know." Mama is folding clothes on the couch and watching TV while Judge Judy is telling someone to "talk only to me!" I hope Judy calls someone out and shouts *Baloney!* I love it when she does that. Or maybe I won't now because it will remind me of a food item we don't have.

"Only one box of mac and cheese."

"I know."

"No more bread."

"Mysti, I know. I'm working on a solution." Mama crumples the shirt in her hands. She tries not to cry.

"And the birthday cake for Laura?" Laura's birthday is coming up and if that kid doesn't get a cake, there will be no living with her.

"Mysti! Please!"

"I'm sorry," I say.

Mama takes the crumpled shirt and folds it smooth as sheets. If Dad was here, he'd rub her shoulders and say, *Oh, Melly, it will be all right, I'll finish these clothes while you go take a bubble bath.*

But I don't do that because it feels weird.

And I fear her solution will have something to do with turnips. They are popping up in the backyard now and if memory serves, Mama thinks you can make a soup of them. News flash: You can't. Or, you shouldn't.

Okay.

"That's baloney!" Judge Judy shouts at a defendant.

I glance at Mama and smile. "No baloney, either."

Mama whips me playfully with a shirt. "Well, maybe I can interest you in some dog food. I heard you served it to your sister."

That little brat told on me!

"Oh, I have homework to do! See ya!"

Three red checks on the calendar later, I'm riding the bus to school and we pass Woman Who Goes Somewhere. She wears orange pants and a yellow top and looks like a walking candy corn, which I take as a good sign. I could stare at her longer for more clues, but I'm in need of an egg. Three eggs to be precise. You can steal toilet paper from Beatty Middle School, but not eggs.

"Can I borrow something?" I asked Rama on the bus.

"Sure."

"Do you have three eggs at home?"

"Well, probably."

"I need them."

"What for?"

"Oh, never mind," I said nervously. "I just wanted to see if you'd say yes."

I didn't want to tell her I needed eggs for a secret birthday cake. Then I'd have to tell her about Mama and the secret and the pamphlets because she would have a thousand questions. I'm just not ready for that yet because we haven't crossed that friendship threshold.

"Sometimes you're weird, Mysti Murphy."

"What can I say, it's a gift."

"That keeps on giving."

"Touché."

"Have you forgotten about that Gomez boy?"

"Who?"

"You know."

"See, I've already forgotten!"

"See you tomorrow! Go, Bears!"

Beatty Middle School Bears. I'd soon be forgetting about them, too.

It's the next day of school. The day I forgot all about Beatty Middle School Bears.

The good thing about today at school is that there is no last-period Texas History class to endure with the hip and not-so-hip and Ms. Overstreet giving us a pop quiz. Mr. Red already took care of that agony earlier in the day when he tested us on our knowledge of the Pythagorean theorem. When I will *ever* use this theorem in real life is beyond me. The bad thing about today is that there is a pep rally during last period and because I am one of the few Beatty Middle School students who forgot to be obsessed with the colors blue and white, I will be on an island where Sandy Showalter and everyone like her will not talk to me. And in case a student should forget, all through the halls there are posters and cheer signs to remind us that we are the Beatty Bears. Mr. Red walks down the hall in his Bear costume, holding the giant Bear head under one arm as he walks. He looks nefarious.

And there are the blue-ribbon girls. Walking. Swaying. Smiling. Holding the cheer signs and clapping their way to the gym. Wayne Kovok, dressed in blue, walks behind them dizzy with happiness like an entourage of one. He probably likes pep-rally day the way I like clean-sheet day.

"Miss Murphy, aren't you going to the pep rally where there will be cheers and shouts and school spirit that will wash away your homework blues forevermore, that is, if you have homework blues or blues of any kind you'd like to talk about in my office, where I have newly upholstered green chairs?" It is the counselor, Ms. Peet, who really needs to become familiar with verbal punctuation. I think my hair grew a full inch in the time it took her to finish talking.

"I would like to sit in your new green chair if you don't mind," I say. It is the only way I know to get out of going to the pep rally. I would rather read anyway. I just checked out a novel about kids who were genetically engineered to survive underwater, and would like to spend some time in a place where that makes sense. So Ms. Peet and I go to her office and I tell her I just need to be quiet if that's all right.

I read my book and Ms. Peet types on her computer as fast as she speaks. After a while, I hear a roar of laughter come from the gym and wish I knew what it was. Sometimes Mr. Red goes really wild with his mascot routine. It's hard to concentrate on my book, so I read a bunch of the posters plastered along Ms. Peet's walls. There are enough for a less sophisticated reader like Laura to spend at least a half hour on. My favorite is I AM IN CHARGE OF HOW I FEEL AND TODAY I CHOOSE HAPPINESS.

At the bus line, Rama, who wisely wore a Beatty Middle School Blue scarf today, tugs my sleeve. "I saw you ditch the pep rally."

"I am in charge of how I feel and today I choose happiness."

"Are you feeling okay?"

"Sure. Hey, what was all that big laugh about during the pep rally?"

"I don't want to tell you."

"Why?"

"It involves the Gomez boy."

"Did he impress somebody?"

"Everyone but me."

"Well, you are hard to impress, Rama," I say. "So what happened?"

"I heard that girl who wears the horse shirt telling the whole story. Anibal is a vocabulary vandal."

Apparently, on Monday in Anibal's Language Arts class, Mr. Vern had written the week's vocabulary list on the board. The third word was *circumspect*, but when Mr. Vern wasn't looking, Anibal changed the word to *circumcise*. Today, when the first three classes turned in their vocabulary quizzes, Mr. Vern got wise and canceled the quizzes for the rest of the day. Half the seventh grade had Anibal to thank for a vocabulary-free afternoon.

Anibal the cool hipster. Score.

Rama gets off the bus and bounces home, which happens to be at the opposite end of Fargo Drive from my house. A house with green shutters and a girl with the supercool name *RamaKhan!* was there all the time and I didn't know it. Dad never drove down our street in that direction. Storm clouds come from that direction. Woman Who Goes Somewhere comes from that direction. I've always thought of that unexplored end of the street as part mystery, part danger.

The wind sweeps up the Raw Sienna leaves from that direction and pushes them down the block.

I wish for more leaves. More leaves on the street means we are closer to October. Closer to Halloween and the time when the red checks on the calendar can stop, and when Mama says she is fine, she will really mean it.

chapter 18

Here is a girl in search of eggs.

Monday.

Squeak. The turn of Mama's door opening. Mama shuffles out, her dirty hair all pulled back in a ponytail. You can see a Warm Gray stripe of color framing her face, marking the difference in what God gave her and the color the box gives her.

"Laura!" she announces with cheer. Faux cheer.

"Happy birthday! I see you got your present, you sneaky mouse."

"Thank you, Mama."

Laura holds a framed certificate declaring that a star has been named for Laura Dawn Murphy in the Carina

Dwarf galaxy. I got the same present when I turned eight, and it was the only time I've ever liked my name. Ever.

"Mysti, can I speak with you?"

Mama tells me to go and see about borrowing eggs from the Jenningses.

"I think I have all the ingredients we need here except for eggs," she whispers.

We both know she hates to do this because she's embarrassed that she can't go to the store herself. Like they don't already know that a woman who can't go see her sick husband in the hospital can't go buy eggs at the store.

"Great idea, Mama!" I, too, sound faux in my cheer. This is us, trying to be fine.

Mama gives me some tomatoes and green onions from our garden as a trade, and I'm out the sliding-glass back door. I wind through the garden, past the evil tree, and up the Jenningses' driveway. This is where I stop. The garage door is open and there is an interesting smell in the air. Not interesting in an *Oh, that smells tasty* kind of way. More of an *Oh, someone spilled a ton of nail polish* kind of way.

"Hey, neighbor," shouts Mr. Jennings. "What's the good word?"

Egg. Egg is the word.

"Nothing," I say.

"Whenever the missus says nothing, it usually means something," he says.

"Actually, I want to know if I can borrow some eggs. We just ran out. I have tomatoes for you."

"Hand me that hammer, will you?"

"What are you trying to build?" I am desperate now to know the source of all the mysterious sounds and nefarious smells. There are at least two tables set up in the garage with a variety of parts and tools, all things that looked like they could go in a car or a computer or a kitchen. A few are laid out on a white cloth like a surgeon lays out his instruments.

"Two great inventions, Mysti. Both with the power to create harmonious marriages and a nice retirement nest."

"But I thought you worked as a mechanic," I say. "Why start inventing now?"

Mr. Jennings looks at me like I've asked the strangest question in the history of question asking.

"Oh, my girl, you have to read all about the great Steve Jobs, like I told you," he says. "He had a drive to create something new and different. He had a drive inside that told him he was special. All inventors possess those same attributes. You have to let it flourish."

By now, Mrs. Jennings has come out into the garage and is shaking her head at her husband.

"He's giving you the sermon, I see," she says. "Well, he's like the Great Wall of China. Impressive but meandering. Your lunch is almost ready, Thomas Edison."

I ask her about the three eggs and she turns to run back into the house.

"She'll see," Mr. Jennings says. "She'll be a believer! I'll be on the Home Shopping Network and she'll understand then."

"With your collapsible measuring cup?" Mrs. Jennings asks over her shoulder. "I don't think so."

"You don't realize how many marriages this will save!" Mr. Jennings says, then turns to me. "Every time I open that cabinet, a thousand plastic measuring cups fall down on my head. So this collapsible contraption—I'm calling it the Amazing Multimeasurer—is going to be hotter than sliced bread!"

You have to like Mr. Jennings. He has hope. There is probably a whole story going on inside his brain all the time.

Here is a girl watching another character in another story.

Mr. Jennings reaches for the thick copy of his biography of Steve Jobs. "There's a passage in this book where young Mr. Jobs realized that he knew more than his father. That was a great turning point for him. I, too, felt that way about my former boss. It's hard for a sapling to grow under someone else's shade. Get what I mean? You have to keep starting sentences with questions. Know what I mean?"

"I think I know someone like that," I say, thinking of Wayne Kovok. "He's a dork at school. Maybe I should tell him to read that book. I think he could relate."

Mr. Jennings winks. "Take it from a fellow dork, kid. Today's dorks are tomorrow's inventors."

"I'd like to see that when it's done," I say. "I would buy it in a hot second."

"Oh, of course, Miss Mur—"

"Okay!" Mrs. Jennings interrupts. "Here are your eggs, dear. Now you tell your mother that if there's anything we can do, just give us a ring and I'll send Mr. Invention right over."

I take myself back home, walking slowly, thinking about how much mystery and movement stirs around me. Woman Who Goes Somewhere takes daily walks in bad clothes to some unknown destination. Dad is in the hospital trying to get better each day. And right next door, some invention with the power to change marriages is being generated in Mr. Jennings's garage. With all of that, maybe the Anibal Gomez experiment isn't so bad. Everyone I know is trying to get to somewhere or get better. That's all Anibal is trying to do, too. I am just part of a hypothesis that he's trying to prove. A variable. A person can be ignored if she knows she is doing it in the service of science. This is what I tell myself. This experiment, like all science experiments, has parameters. It has rules and an end date. If you know something will eventually come to an end, you can handle it.

In the kitchen, Mama mixes the ingredients for lemon cake. Soon the house smells golden, and it reminds me of the world before the stupid tree changed everything.

When I was little, Mama baked banana bread and I would sit on the counter, staring at the oven glass, watching the batter turn from gooey yellow to golden brown while she braided my hair. I'd have that soft, floaty feeling inside from her hands working through my red hair, while at the same time smelling the wonder of home-baked bread.

I loved that part of my story. I loved it when Mama played that character in our book.

"Mama, about the food situation? I was thinking that I could—"

"I transferred money into your school cafeteria accounts," she says. "And I have a solution that will get us by for the next two weeks. You know, until your dad comes back." She walks to the calendar and checks off another day.

She is still holding on to the optimistic view of Dr. Randolph. She believes that Dad's body knows it's supposed to automatically wake up on October 31 and ask for Halloween candy. As for me, I'm not so sure, because I looked up more facts about coma patients on the Internet. Unless Dad is playing the role of coma patient in a movie, it is unclear if he will really sit up and ask for a candy corn. The Internet says everybody is different. Tell me something I don't know.

"What is your solution?" I ask Mama.

Here is a girl helping her mother unpack the unappetizing contents of an emergency supply kit.
The contents of Mama's solution fit on our couch.
- 12 assorted meals ready to eat (MRE)
- A can opener
- 15 protein bars
- 3 boxes of granola
- 1 jar of peanut butter
- 3 packages of dried fruit
- 1 can of nuts
- 2 boxes of crackers
- 12-pack of canned juice
- 1 box of nonperishable pasteurized milk
- 1 jar of multivitamins

- 1 sleeping bag
- 1 jug of household chlorine bleach
- 1 fire extinguisher
- Matches in a waterproof container
- Feminine hygiene items
- Paper cups and plates, paper towels, and plastic utensils
- Paper and pencil
- 2 puzzles for children

The box doesn't include dog food or toilet paper.

"Apparently you aren't supposed to have a pet or need to pee during an emergency," I say to Mama.

"Or need to color your hair!" Mama laughs. I look at her roots. Dad's been gone a quarter inch at least.

"Well, someone in the government should think of that," I say. "People need to use the bathroom and have nice hair in an emergency."

"Nice hair is not a priority in an emergency," Mama says, a little laugh in her voice. "And the kit *did* have toilet paper, but I believe your dad used it. You know how nervous he got when we ran low."

How nervous he got.

We both lock eyes. She just talked about Dad in the past tense as if he is already gone. Quick, I see Mama's brain turning, trying to clean up what she said out loud.

"Well, we'll laugh about this when your dad is home in a few weeks. He'll be back before there is a true emergency," Mama says, leaning into the word *true*. "And the garden will sustain us."

I knew it. Turnips will be part of this plan.

"There are ants in these crackers!" Laura says.

"Maybe they had an emergency," I say.

"How did they cross the chalk line?" Laura asks.

There is a giant chalk line around our house. Chalk dust coats every baseboard in our house because Mama read someplace that ants won't crawl over chalk. This is another example of how our family fixes problems. There is the normal way and there is the Murphy family way. Can we get bug man out here to murder these annoying creatures? No way. Instead we pretend that ants are afraid of chalk and that we don't mind white dust everywhere.

"I think I know how the ants crossed." Laura looks at me, pulls me to her room. "You have a *new* story, I can tell."

Here are about one hundred ant leaders. They gathered for an early-morning meeting outside on the sidewalk. Andy Ant, who is the chief, says to the others: Get your troops ready, men! Today we are taking down 4520 Fargo Drive. It's going to be a long mission, going underground and inside the small weep holes, but I know you can do it. Early recon tells us that there are several Cheerios under the refrigerator. The littlest girl dropped a peppermint candy and it's near the garage entry. We'll need delta crew to move that one. So who is with me?

Hurrah! Hurrah! Hurrah! shout the ant leaders in reply.

Then, the ant leaders and their army of thousands encircle 4520 Fargo Drive. They make great progress, doing the army crawl over and under. But then suddenly, the ant leaders panic and shout Turn back! Turn back! Turn back! There's a line of chalk, I repeat, line of chalk. No entry possible. Abort the mission!

And the ants regroup and move down to the next house.

"Mysti, I love your stories." It is Mama who says this. I didn't even know she was listening, because she was all the way in the kitchen. But then, that is how small our house is. Every word is all out there in the open. Except for the things we don't talk about. Like the origins of her fears. If Dad is going to wake up, put on his slippers, and drive straight to Tom Thumb to get groceries.

And how we will get toilet paper and dog food into this house.

I do my homework and then contemplate the still-unfixed crack in my ceiling.

It lengthens.

It moves.

It grows wider.

I don't know if that is significant, except that I do not like spiders and their ability to enter and exit through cracks when I'm not looking.

chapter 19

Here is a girl listening to songs that speak to her soul and staying up too late texting when her parental unit shouts to shut it down.

Are you adjusting your hat?

Some people like it.

Yeah. I heard girls talking about you.

Who?

Not SS

Who?

Try more Axe deodorant

Who? You're killing me! Calling u now.

I let my phone ring three times before answering. Let Anibal sweat it out a little bit. But when I hear his voice and it is a private conversation between two friends, I am happy.

"How's your dad?" Anibal asks, and it makes me realize the old Anibal still lives underneath his stupid new hat and stupid new ironic T-shirts.

"Same. Not worse."

"Coolio. So tell me about these girls already."

"I thought this experiment was all about Sandy."

"It is. But if other ladies are enjoying my hotness, I should know about it."

"I was just kidding," I lie.

"I bet people have said stuff and you just haven't heard it yet. Anyway, I just can't seem to get Sandy's attention," Anibal says.

I was already working on a way to get her attention. I'd seen her trying without success to make a bracelet out of Starburst wrappers. All the girls had them. Her cheer squad friends seemed to be making them every day, and Sandy lagged behind in her skill at folding, which was her only obvious flaw. So I've been working on a shoelace bracelet in the colors of blue and white. Shoelaces I stole out of Dad's presently unused shoes. Shoelaces I will replace when I replace the stolen TP as well. My plan is to finish braiding the bracelet in front of her and get her to notice how easy it is. If I can get her to start the next bracelet trend, I can get a nice friendly text from her, right?

"Here's the thing," I say. "Music. Find out her music."

"Who cares about her music? It's probably not hipster."

121

"Songs say things girls wish they could say."

"Oh. Is that really true?" Anibal asks.

I don't know a lot of girls, but this feels true in my bones so I just say to him, "Yes, it's a universal truth. Songs are a different kind of girl language."

chapter 20

Here is a girl opening a military meal so that her dog can eat two chicken-on-a-bun sandwiches.

Right before lunch, I put a song together in my head.
I want a different life.
My dad is sick.
My dog is hungry.
My mother sleeps a lot.
And my sister, la, la, la, cried herself to sleep last night because she got in the special regional choir and can't accept because there's no one to drive her to practice and even though she's a brat, it made me so mad. So mad because of the subject we don't talk about.
La. La. La.

That's how the song goes. It's called "Put Some Duct Tape on It."

I don't say anything when I sit down at the Island. I just keep my head low and eat my lunch: a spaghetti-and-meat-sauce MRE.

"Did you know those were first issued by the military in 1981 and most have about twelve hundred calories?" Wayne says. Wayne Kovok got very interested in my lunch. I've managed to cleverly conceal the MRE packaging most days, but not today.

"It's part of my science project," I lie. "Try out MREs." This MRE tastes gross. I eat two bites and put it away.

"Wow."

"You're incredible, Wayne," Rama adds.

Wayne blushes for no good reason. Rama's insults fly under his radar sometimes.

Life on the Loser Island continues. It has taken my appetite away and I don't eat.

"You're in Advanced English, too, right?" Wayne asks me.

"Yep."

"Are you doing that poetry block now? I don't get that at all."

"I can help you with it."

"Poetry is not my thing."

"I'm shocked."

I'm making actual conversation at lunch while the sound of Anibal's laughter carries across the cafeteria like a bad song. So I change the channel and pretend Wayne said the funniest thing ever said in a lunchroom.

"Are you okay?" Wayne asks.

Then Anibal Gomez comes by the Loser Island and pretends to be friendly.

"Hey."

"Hey."

"Can you go through the line and buy me lunch today, 'cause I don't have any money?" he asks.

I go through the lunch line and buy Anibal Gomez anything he wants. Who cares. Who cares about those looks from Wayne and Rama. La. La. La.

What we're doing is a secret. No one knows about the Sandy Showalter challenge. If they did, they'd think differently.

I hope I'm in a fairy-tale story where the kind girl gets to sit with her friend, who, after realizing his error, reunites with her over chicken-on-a-bun and two chocolate milks.

"Why are you following me?" he asks.

"Because of the lunch."

"Lunch only, hold the weird girl." Anibal says this stinging barb loud enough for his friends to hear.

Here is a dorky girl who can feel hot waves of immature laughter coming from the vending machine, where the villainous lackeys look on with amusement.

I stand there in a puddle of stupid.

A puddle.

I shake it off and go through the line again and buy a chicken-on-a-bun for Larry. At least that is a small problem I can solve and it gets me paddling away from my puddle of stupidity.

"You still—" Rama says.

"Don't say it. I already know."

"I finally understand. You like him. Like, like him, like him."

"We have history. We're really good friends. He's just kidding around." Maybe I should show her the texts. Proof of friendship.

I wonder if I could explain this to Rama so that it would make sense. No, I don't think that's possible. It's a "You have to be there" kind of friendship. Not being friends with Anibal is like asking a fish not to swim.

Rama says, "Earth to Mysti. What are you thinking now?"

"I'm picturing his head as a giant cantaloupe."

"Yes, that's a good strategy."

"It already looks sort of melon-shaped, don't you think?"

I doodle in my notebook. I rain down insults on Anibal, taking the chance that Ms. Overstreet or Ms. Peet isn't going to ninja-drop into Loser Island and catch me drawing an Anibaloupe.

My drawing looks more like a monkey that swallowed a melon. Well, I never said drawing was my talent.

Rama asks, "Will you help me after school? I keep getting to class late because I can't get my locker to open."

"They do that on purpose to torture the sixth graders."

"It's working. I feel tortured."

"RamaKhan!"

"What?"

"I like saying your name like that," I say. "RamaKhan! Sounds like a superhero. You should say that to yourself if you feel like a tortured sixth grader again."

"MystiMurphy!"

"See, it's not the same."

"Not even close."

Rama walks away and I check my watch. Only a few more hours of this stupid day.

Here is a girl holding out hope that lunchroom humiliation with a side of embarrassment is forgotten by the end of the day.

chapter 21

Here is a girl trying to survive the Texas Revolution.

I sense danger as I enter Texas History. Potential nefariousness. Maybe I just have a bad feeling. Maybe I'm just hungry and wish I had eaten my MRE. Or maybe I've just been watching too many Animal Planet shows about animal instinct in the wild.

Something inside the animal senses danger and it uses this ability to save itself or flee. The animal, for example, senses tiny vibrations underneath the earth. Vibrations that signal an earthquake or a tsunami. That it should not enter a cave or a part of the forest. It just knows.

I think my stomach senses something.

It is gurgling as I head into Texas History. It tells me:

Do not go into this cave. I chalk it up as simple hunger. (Later, I will tell my stomach I was wrong and it was right.)

But right now Ms. Overstreet strolls up and down the aisles of the class trying to get us to focus on the siege of the Alamo.

"Please tell me some of the major heroes of this battle," Ms. Overstreet says.

Wayne's hand shoots up like a rocket and he rolls off the usual suspects and is rewarded with a smile from Sandy Showalter.

Ms. Overstreet reaches for her Texas-shaped pointer and aims it at the board.

"Wake up, the story gets better. I want you to write all of this down and commit it to memory, cowgirls and cowboys!"

Ms. Overstreet starts her engine and doesn't stop. I fill my notebook page as fast as I can. I don't want to give her any reason to suspect I'm an undercover bully, now do I?

Here is what I write.

1700s—Spanish built Alamo as a mission
Texas was part of Mexico at this time, wanted independence.
Dec. 1835—Group of Texas volunteers fought Mexican soldiers in San Antonio, won, and occupied the Alamo.

Mexican government mad. Angry as hornets.

Feb. 1836—General Santa Anna arrives to stop rebellion. Game on, Texans!

Battle of Alamo. 145 Texas defenders against 6,000 Mexican soldiers.

Fought valiantly for 13 days.

The Alamo reclaimed by the Mexican army.

But the stand gave Sam Houston time to organize a bigger army. Remember the Alamo!

Sam Houston and his new army went on to defeat Santa Anna at the battle of San Jacinto.

In conclusion—Don't mess with Texas!

"Did you get all that, cowgirls and cowboys? Why was the battle so inspiring?" Ms. Overstreet booms.

I stare at my notebook. My notebook knows more about the Texas Revolution than I do. Seriously, it could pass a test.

"Because it wasn't a fair fight at all. It would be like our Beatty Middle School team being forced to play against the Dallas Cowboys by sending the orchestra onto the field! Very unfair. And yet, the orchestra, holding their violas and violins, *still* manages to score one touchdown! This is what makes the battle of the Alamo so awe-inspiring. The Texans fought against all odds. And it is their courage we celebrate when we say *Remember the Alamo!*"

I would be more engaged in her talk right now, because she is really, really going at this subject with something close to a full-on nerd rage. But my guts are gurgling and rumbling. It's hard to follow history and inspiration on an empty stomach, even when you have a boot-wearing teacher standing on her desk. So I stare at the life-size poster of Sam Houston hanging on the wall. There is a quote above Houston's head:

DO THE RIGHT THING AND BEAR THE CONSEQUENCES!

"Okay, let's have a pop quiz!"

Groans from the class. Growls from my stomach.

Why did you go into this cave? the stomach asks.

"Don't fear, this is just an oral quiz to see if you heard anything or if I was just performing for the sake of my own enjoyment. Okay, Miss Showalter, can you please tell me the original name of the Alamo?"

Sandy does not answer. She chews the end of her pencil.

Ms. Overstreet repeats herself in what can only be described as a constipated voice.

Slow and slightly clenched.

"It was Mission San Antonio de Valero." Of course, Sandy's rescuer is Wayne Kovok. He is granted another nice Sandy smile for saving her from the land of no answers.

"And in what month did Santa Anna arrive in San Antonio and surround the Alamo?" Ms. Overstreet asks.

"February 1836," Anibal states. "He caught them by surprise!"

"Good. And the Texans held out in the Alamo for thirteen days, fighting Santa Anna's army in the dead of winter," Ms. Overstreet continues. "I'd like you all to consider this question: What makes a hero? Is a hero someone who performs a valiant act? Is a hero someone who doubles her resolve during a difficult situation?"

"Did you know the word *hero* is derived from the Greek and means 'protector' or 'defender'?" says Wayne Kovok.

"I wonder what that would have been like for the defenders of the Alamo," Ms. Overstreet states. "Can you imagine the feeling? The fear? The courage? You know, I like what the famous essayist Ralph Waldo Emerson had to say about a hero. Do you want to know what he said?

"He said that 'a hero is no braver than an ordinary man, but he is brave five minutes longer.' Five minutes longer! Have you ever been in a situation where you gave up? What if you stayed with that difficulty five minutes longer? Does anyone have any thoughts on this?"

I turn my head to Anibal and the look on his face is one I recognize. It is the "I will not be outdone" face. It is the "I will use my brain to prevail" face. The face that used to help him succeed using his brain alone.

"Well, to quote the lyrics of a Taylor Swift song," Anibal begins. I don't hear the rest of what Anibal says because my brain came to a full stop on the words *Taylor Swift*.

Anibal just quoted Taylor Swift to answer a Texas History question.

Wait, Anibal just quoted Taylor Swift to answer a Texas History question?

Anibal Gomez found a way to worm song lyrics into a discussion of Texas revolutionaries to impress a girl. If I wasn't so annoyed that I gave him that clue, I'd be impressed.

"Very interesting, Mr. Gomez," Ms. Overstreet says. "Let us consider this question more deeply. Miss Murphy, what do you think of Emerson's definition?"

Here is a girl who regrets thinking of lemon cake and not paying attention to the teacher.

"Do you believe Mr. Emerson was right about his meaning of a hero? That a hero is no braver than an ordinary man, but he is brave five minutes longer?"

I have the attention of the entire class, all of their collective, inquiring eyes on me.

"We're waiting, Miss Murphy."

She waits.

I wait.

I wait to spontaneously combust right here in Texas History.

Which would make history.

"I agree with Mr. Emerson," I say finally, because there are only two options: Agree or disagree, and I'm gambling I've chosen wisely.

"Well, can you expand on your answer?" Ms. Overstreet says.

Do you know what happens? My stomach answers.

Not a tiny, look-over-your-shoulder-and-giggle growl. A *large*, powerful, noticeable growl. Almost like an animal. A growl heard around Texas History, probably into Social Studies next door, possibly into Mr. Red's class, too.

"It takes courage to show up," Wayne says quickly. "And then to stay. I think that's a decent definition of a hero. A lot of the guys at the Alamo could have gone. Did you know Santa Anna didn't seal the exits immediately? They could have left. But they stayed."

I look to Wayne and mouth the words, *Thank you*. I won't be so hard on him with all of his "Did you know" factoids now.

Anibal grins at his perceived victory. And why not? Sandy is all smiles and chewing on her pencil because she is surrounded by guys who like her.

chapter 22

Here is a girl who wishes this day was just a dream.

The stomach has spoken!!

Not.

They call u Texas History Growler

Who does?

Just me.

Right now!!!! ☺

Taylor Swift? Really?

Been waitin to use that all day!

Boosh!

Get ur own ideas next time.

Growl!

Shut up.

Dad? Home?

Still in hospital.

Dude!

I know, right?

chapter 23

Here is a girl drawing a small green dragon in the margins of her math notebook, wishing dragons were real and kind and a form of transportation.

Math.

Math has been a safe place for me the past couple of days. Only one person called me the Texas History Growler yesterday and we already know what wannabe-hipster brain came up with that.

"Okay, let's get ready to *rhombusssss!*"

Mr. Red.

He tries so hard to make math cool. But in the end, he's still a teacher who chews toothpicks and reads the sports pages while we take pop quizzes to determine if we can tell polygons from pizza.

Today Mr. Red has pie-plate-sized sweat stains under his armpits, which oddly led to thoughts of how to be noticed in middle school by ignoring old friends and acting stupid with new ones. I haven't said anything to Anibal about his being a jerk, as Rama keeps reminding me. Every day, she stands there in the safe girls' restroom, one hand on her hip and a scowl on her face.

"You keep saying the nice Anibal Gomez is going to show up. News flash, he's late!" she complains. And then I think of future days when the three of us will all fall over laughing at how funny this first semester of school has been and how I was in on the joke the whole time.

Here is a girl who may be kidding herself.

Now I've opened the door and told the thoughts to please leave, but they insist on staying like a song you can't get out of your head.

"Who can tell me which of these is a rhombus?" asks Mr. Red. "Anyone?"

No one.

Mr. Red is interrupted midphrase by the sound of the loudspeaker. It isn't the regular morning announcements because they'd already informed us that for lunch you could get an oven-baked chicken patty with whole wheat bun and seasoned green beans, which I'd drawn a sketch of in my notebook. The chicken patty features legs and the green beans danced. I figure if I get caught, there is no chance any teacher can find it offensive, with the possible exception of a vegetarian.

"Attention, students and teachers," Principal Blakely announces. "Unfortunately, we've had a serious mechanical problem with the air-conditioning and must cancel the remainder of the school day. We've made the decision to let students leave by midday. The buses will run at twelve thirty. Other students can call their parents if they are not riding the bus. We have reasonable expectations that this problem will be corrected today and classes will resume tomorrow. Thank you."

I have reasonable expectations that this problem will work in my favor. I can check one miserable day off my school survival calendar and spend the rest of the day reading at home. Suddenly, the oppressive heat is a Get Out of Jail Free card.

Mr. Red's entire class moves like a herd of slow cattle. Jokes are whispered. Jokes about sweat stains growing into octagons. By twelve thirty the whole school is outside in that beat-down heat known as Texas under the sun. The sky is colorless and dry and looks brittle as a blanket that's been on the clothesline too long. Across the parking lot, you can make out a wavy mirage.

Whose idea was it to go ahead and line us up early

for the buses, I have no idea. This time delay wouldn't be so bad if Anibal Gomez and his faux friends weren't in line, too, with their new green sneakers and overspray of Axe.

I'm careful not to make eye contact with him, but I feel his presence and smell his attempts at sweaty subterfuge.

Here is a girl who can't tell if the heat on her back is from the sun or the penetrating stare of Boy Who Sleeps on Stuffed Animals.

Anibal mocks some kid's sneakers for how worn-out they are. He takes his hat off and keeps adjusting his hair.

Rama gets into our bus line. Man, she must be hot with that scarf on her head. I wonder why she doesn't take it off, let her hair breathe a little bit.

"There's the Sand Girl," one of Anibal's friends snaps. I hear the echo of Anibal's laughter in the crowd. Not only are their insults stupid, they're repetitive.

"Hey, Mysti, maybe you could get a scarf and put it over your teeth." This is Anibal's clever friend. I name him Boy Who Should Disappear.

Where is the stupid bus?

Where is Ms. Peet and her buttons about bullying? Why is it that those who most need to get caught somehow slip through the cracks of authority?

The crack is narrow.

Boy Who Should Disappear makes more jabs at Rama.

140

He calls her Osama Rama. Ouch! Then he looks at me. He calls me the Texas History Growler. So much laughter. So little presence of teachers. So much injustice.

Rama tugs my sleeve. "Let's walk."

"I can't."

"Something wrong with your feet?"

There is a joke Dad likes to tell. What has four legs but can't walk?

A chair.

A chair can't walk and neither can I.

It takes the bus seventeen minutes to get from the school to Fargo Drive. But I've never walked home from Beatty Middle School.

I've never walked farther than the distance from the bus stop to my own brown front door. And it occurs to me right at this moment that even in the car with Dad, I've never even left my stupid ZIP code!

"Sorry, I can't," I say, feeling a little as if I'm letting her down.

But I can't let Mama down, either.

Rama starts walking and when she does, she cuts a defiant image. *RamaKhan!*

Anibal shouts, "Go with your Sand Girl friend, Missed-teeth. And walk all the way to the dentist." I look at him and he winks. As if insulting someone and then adding a wink takes away the sting.

There is a ruffle of laughter.

Someone tells them to shut up. I don't know who, but wish I could hug them. "What if we cut your hair?" Boy Who Should Disappear says. A piece of paper hits my head. "Go borrow a scarf from her."

Where are the stupid buses?

"I am going to cut your hair when you're not looking," Boy Who Should Disappear says.

I think of those stupid animal shows again and know an animal would not sit around and take this abuse. Seriously, when do you ever see an animal sit there while another pelts it with rocks or coconuts? Animals are smart. An animal would flee. So I flee. I will try to catch up with Rama even though she is no longer in view.

Easy.

It hasn't been that long, has it? She'd rounded a curve and I don't see her, but I can catch up, right?

I hear the shouts of the boys, all making chicken sounds.

Bok. Bok. Bok.

I don't care. They can stay in the heat. Melt into the concrete. Let people walk over them for eternity.

Here is a girl using her imagination to magically turn each of the boys into a chicken patty with whole wheat bun and beat them about the head with seasoned green beans.

I focus on the sidewalk until I get around the corner of the parking lot, moving one foot at a time. Any moment now, I will see the back of Rama's head. I will follow her until we reach Fargo Drive.

Easy.

Man, if I had Sandy Showalter's phone number, I could put a stop to this right now. I could tell her how great Anibal is. *Sandy, you could study Texas History together and Anibal would help you with your science project. He likes frozen yogurt, too. He has several younger brothers and sisters and is very good with them. He gets cool posters from the dollar store. Call him now before some other cheer squad girl gets him.*

Yes, I could find her number, tell her these things, and we'd have a great laugh. She would thank me and then all this social experiment would be at an end. Even Rama would come to know the good side of Anibal.

And then, when this is all straightened out, I can figure out a way to make Mama happy. Happier. I can ask Anibal to bring food from the dollar store. They have milk there. Bread. Basic things. Even toilet paper and shoelaces. I can give him my Christmas money and he can bring little items a few at a time. It will be a small thing, but it will help out a lot until Dad comes home.

Perfect. Perfect plans.

The thing about making perfect plans in a fantasy world of your own mind is that when you reenter the real world, you may realize that you are lost.

And you realize that you are so stupid to flee like an animal because animals do not spend so much time thinking, do they? No, they probably just run to another part of the forest, find a shady spot to sit, and call it home.

Here is a girl experiencing nine shades of nefariousness.
Lost.
Lost in my own stupid town.
Okay, think, Mysti. You've ridden the bus for a year. You've got to figure this out. You've got to get home before Mama panics.
Mama.

She will suffer the most from my being lost. Or snatched? And Laura alone with Mama? That is a dreadful thought. Mama will never let Laura go back to school. They will both be forced to survive on tap water and turnips. They will wear those HAVE YOU SEEN ME? T-shirts until my iron-on photo fades away.

The first thing my non-animal brain does is some kind of mental blame equation that adds up all the reasons this is not *my* fault.

If Texas wasn't so hot, the school AC would not have broken.

And then students wouldn't have to go home early.

Making the buses really disorganized.

And if the buses weren't disorganized, there wouldn't be a long line of jerks with more insults than sense.

And insults make you walk away.

You wouldn't have to walk if your mom drove or dear old Dad wasn't sick.

And Dad wouldn't be sick if not for the stupid dumb old tree.

I line up this equation in my mind. The common denominator of blazing heat and old tree is Mother Nature. And since nature is created by God, I look to the sky and begin to lay the ultimate blame heavenward. Right as I am deciding between saying a prayer or shouting an insult, I hear a voice call out to me:

"Mysti, you are not lost. You are just confused."

chapter 24

It is not the voice of God I hear. It is the voice of a girl with a scarf, and a hand on her hip.

Here is a girl who knows that animals help each other in the wild.

"What are you talking about?" I say. "I know I'm not lost!"

"Well, don't be a slowpoke. It's hot out here."

"What's your phone number?" I ask Rama. All my panic could have easily vanished if I had her phone number. On the walk home, we exchange numbers. Then I try to memorize the way home. I discover that all the streets in my neighborhood are cleverly alphabetized. Atlanta. Boston. El Dorado. Fargo.

Fargo!

I kick an acorn as we walk. "Try not to let their stupidity bother you."

"When I'm a famous doctor, I will not save them from cancer."

"Agreed!"

As we turn down Fargo, I feel the aftershocks of being afraid and lost still rattling my bones. That's the closest real danger I've ever experienced. My legs are filled with nervous energy. They want to rest and sprint at the same time.

"Where did you go?" Rama asks.

"What?"

"Your face. It looked like it went someplace far away."

"Well, I'm back now."

"Want to watch me needlepoint?"

"Needlepoint?"

"It's practice for surgery."

"So you're going to be a surgeon and cure cancer?"

"You say that like it's something strange."

"No, not strange. It's unusual. It rocks."

Rama goes inside her house and I sit on her porch until she comes back outside with her mother.

Like Rama, Mrs. Khan wears a neat head scarf and an expression of concern.

"So you are staying out here?" her mother asks.

"For a while if that's okay," Rama answers. "This is Mysti."

I say hi.

"Let me know if you get too hot," Rama's mother says. "Nice to meet you, Mysti. Rama, we leave for practice at four."

She closes the door and I see Rama rolling her eyes. "Sorry I didn't invite you in. She doesn't want the 'real world' coming into our house and messing with our culture."

"How would I mess with your culture?"

"Who knows, but apparently having a sleepover with someone could change my religion," Rama says. "Hey, what is the Krusty Krab and why does it need so many managers?"

"What?"

"On Facebook. Everyone says they work as a fry cook at the Krusty Krab."

"You're on Facebook?" First, there is the shock of being lost. Second, there is the shock of Rama Khan on Facebook.

"Since I can't have sleepovers and am forced to attend Saturday math tutoring *and* be a violin genius, I negotiated with my mother that I could look at it for two hours a week."

I want to say, *Wow, that is really weird,* but I don't. I'm someone who is constantly pretending I'm in Paris or making up horrible songs about my life, so who am I to judge.

"Rama, are you familiar with that classic show *SpongeBob*?"

"No."

"It's a cartoon, silly." While Rama needlepoints a yellow flower into white cloth, I provide her with basic cartoon knowledge (Bikini Bottom) and what *tbh* means (to be honest) and my dad's personal theory of why people post all about their life on Facebook (because they are not living one). She seems obsessed with understanding Facebook and the acronyms of boys. I try to tell her that Facebook isn't cool anymore, but she won't listen.

"They don't even spell actual words correctly. *Girl* is with an *i*, not g-u-r-l."

"Then don't look at it."

"So you'll help me? And don't make fun of me?"

"Who said I'd make fun of you?" *Not to your face.*

Rama's intelligence has intimidated me from the first day I met her, so it's nice to know she's not perfect.

"RamaKhan!"

"RamaKhan!"

After a while, guess who walks past? Woman Who Goes Somewhere cruising on down Fargo Drive. Today she wears a yellow corduroy jacket, baggy jeans, and giant white-framed sunglasses.

"What do you think of her, Rama?"

"Well, she's no hipster!"

We roll on the ground laughing.

Rama's mother pokes her head out the front door again, so I take it as a sign to stop endangering her daughter's culture. I get to the curb in front of 4520 Fargo Drive and regard our house. It looks extra brown and extra plain.

Inside, it's so quiet and still and there is no one to talk to. No one to say, *Hey, guess what, I walked home. How about that?* Mama's door is big and closed so I tiptoe around so that she can sleep. I don't even take a shower, which is what I really want to do.

I hide in the office and spend time researching how not to get lost in your own neighborhood.

Here is how you do that research.

You search online and gather maps and directions and study them like you're having a test at school and the grade will count for the whole year. It's pass or fail. That's how hard you study. When you're done, you know the distance it will take to travel to the places you need to go. You know how long it will take to get there. You tell yourself it won't be as scary now that you're more prepared. You feel a little better. Your bones and legs feel a little less shaky.

From our house to Beatty Middle School: 1.2 miles, twenty-five-minute walk.

From our house to Tom Thumb grocery store: 0.9 miles, twenty minutes.

And then you look up the map to your dream location even though there's no possible way to walk there. Unless your dreams had feet.

From our house to Paris, France: 4,928 miles, forever.

Finally, you print out all this information, take it to your room, and slip it between the books propping up your bed. You hope the information will seep into your brain while you sleep.

chapter 25

Here is a girl texting the only person who wouldn't mock her for being in middle school and preparing for a distant future.

Hey

Hey!

What r u doing?

Homework. U?

Same. Studying.

Have question.

?

I think u should forget about Gomez.

Why do you care?

U R my friend.

☺

☻

Still. Don't care about him anymore. Even Wayne agrees

Wayne!!!!

Wayne. So forget him.

You should get to know him.

Maybe. I think u should like Wayne.

Wayne!!??

His FB status says he's reading.

LOL. Of course it does!

What does to mack on someone mean? Sandy is doing this.

OMG!

Forget Gomez boy! Forget wannabe hipsters.

Good night!

Rama doesn't understand about Anibal. Anibal doesn't understand Rama. That is the truth. All the time, I hear Dad say that people are as different as apples and oranges. Anibal and Rama are the apples and oranges of my life.

Anibal is trying to change the best he knows how. Trying not to be last year's Anibal, who was round and teased and tortured over his weight. The Anibal no one would really talk to. Except me. I'm still the same and still wanting to talk to him. But he's gone and become something different. I am not so completely stupid that I agree with his methods. And Rama is trying to change and make herself better, too. They are both running toward change. They don't consider it a scary monster.

Well, how long can a person truly stay the same? Isn't the universe even designed to change with each season? Leaves morph from tiny green buds into beautiful hand-sized sheets and then on to reds and browns and golds. Girls who are frightened become girls who can walk a mile and a half. Mothers who paint keep painting over perfectly good walls and canvases because they want to picture something new.

We are all changing beings.

Now that I am in bed, safe under my soft and warm comforter, I do not want to ever leave. Here is a space where there are no problems. Only the crack in my ceiling. That is the only problem. A crack that widens because maybe the house wants to change, too. So there are no problems.

Except for the problems you carry in your mind. They creep into your safe space without an invitation. This problem is so stupid there is not even a name for it. Because what do you call that irritating feeling that tells you you're going to have to change whether you want to or not? What do you call these invisible things that seem like they are marching toward you and you better get ready? What is that?

Larry rolls over, lets out a soft growl. I let my arm fall off the bed and pet him.

"I know, boy, I know. I just need a sign. If I have a sign, it will be enough of a push to keep moving. We can't both be growlers."

If I don't do something about all this, I tell you I will become more like Mama, less like Dad. More like someone who stays home and paints the world. Less like a person who sees the world.

Right now, the thing to do is make a plan. Step one, make friends with Sandy by giving her the braided shoelace bracelet. Stick close to Rama and Wayne. And make sure that I eat enough at lunch so that my days as the Texas History Growler are behind me. Be like an animal and listen to my instincts, but don't think so much that you get lost. And do as Rama suggested and avoid wannabe hipsters.

That's all I have to do.

Here is a girl with the shaky sensation of having a foot on two boats. She must quickly decide which way to jump before the expanding water makes the decision for her and she falls into splashy doom.

chapter 26

Here is a girl convincing herself that everything will be okay if she avoids chicken-on-a-bun and wannabe hipsters.

You cannot avoid wannabe-hipster friends when your sinister Texas History teacher pairs you together for a project. Man, this class wants to kill my hope, one humiliation at a time.

Today, Ms. Overstreet enters from the back of the room.

Her boots click against the floor, making this sound as she walks: *new-evil-plan-new-evil-plan-new-evil-plan.*

"You are going to be excited about this next assignment on the Texas Revolution, which you will complete by working in groups of two," she says. "Your mission, should you choose to accept it, is to never forget the Alamo! In order to do this, you will create the Alamo!"

She arrives at her desk and smiles a conspiratorial half-smile. I know it's not to conceal her teeth. She has perfect teeth the way most villains do. She scans the classroom and calls out names, pairing the two people least likely to want to work together on a project.

Evil.

She has to know poor non-Proactiv-affording, trombone-playing Wayne Kovok has a crush on Sandy Showalter.

"Sandy Showalter and ... Wayne Kovok."

And she goes on.

Ms. Overstreet prepares to pair another set of seventh graders with dire consequences. She announces, "How about Mysti Murphy and ... Anibal Gomez."

According to Ms. Overstreet, Anibal Gomez and I can work together to create a Texas Revolution project.

According to me, we cannot.

In the past, you would have seen me grin with excitement and consider all the great conversations we'd have while doing a project together. Not today.

"But Ms. Overstreet—" I say.

"No, I'm not assigning *new* partners, Mysti," she says in a voice that suggests I've insulted her ability to teach just by partially raising my hand. I have my doubts as to whether Ms. Overstreet was ever a seventh-grade student. Her memory of what it takes to survive has vanished.

"Each project will be due in three weeks. You will present in pairs to the class. You are to identify the major heroes of the Texas Revolution and create a booklet or PowerPoint presentation of your results. You are to write an essay on the qualities of a hero. And, you're to construct a replica of the Alamo. You'll have the final fifteen minutes of each class period to work with your partner. Your time starts now."

Of course, I'm the first to make a move toward Anibal Gomez.

"Hey."

"Hey."

With this kind of epic conversation, what can go wrong?

A lot.

"You can pretty much do this," Anibal says.

"No way."

"It hurts my feelings to do the Alamo," he says. "Those were my people."

Even *more* reason you should help. For your people."

"You get started and I'll think about it."

"Well, don't injure yourself thinking."

"What's your problem?"

Ms. Overstreet passes by our desks and asks how we are doing.

"Fine," Anibal says. "Buy me lunch tomorrow and I'll work on it a little bit."

"I'm not falling for that again."

I fell for it again.

But if you knew my trick, you wouldn't roll your eyes to China like Rama did. She didn't know that I got back at Anibal in my own special way. I made him a one-of-a-kind sandwich.

"I'll get your lunch, just go sit down."

Right after I pay for his chicken-on-a-bun, I sink three pieces of Larry's dog food deep into the patty and then replace the bun. It's the last of my lunch money, but I don't mind.

"Here's your sandwich."

"Here's the list and some supplies my mom got at the dollar store." Anibal hands me a list of the famous figures in the Texas Revolution and a jumbo package of Popsicle sticks, and tells me to go sit someplace else, his friends are coming. Three dollars and seventy-five cents of my lunch account went to a few supplies and a piece of paper I could've found on my own. And a menu selection called Larry's Revenge.

I call that a bargain.

Here is a girl watching an oblivious boy eat dog chow.

Later, he walks by the Island and one of his stupid friends hits Wayne in the back of his head.

"Sorry, Dorkvok," Anibal says.

I want to say that if you insist on being a jerk, you will be forced to eat a secret ingredient. But I don't. I watched him eat every stupid crumb and then I told Rama about my trick. For once, the mention of Anibal Gomez puts a smile on her face.

"Come with me," I say to her, because I need her help with the Sandy Showalter bracelet surprise.

We toss our trash and I head toward the mean girls' restroom.

"Wait!" Rama says.

"If you don't come inside with me, I'll understand."

"What is all this about?"

"It's about ending something that never should have started."

"Clearer, please," Rama says. I consider telling her about Anibal's crush on Sandy and how she's the one missing hipster accessory he still doesn't have. I consider spilling all the beans about the social experiment and how I've agreed to be publicly humiliated. Maybe she would consider it an exchange for more acronyms and Facebook knowledge. But just lining up the right words in my brain makes the whole thing sound as pathetic as it is. And I really hope she will like Anibal once this is all over and done with. So I just say, "I'm going to give Sandy Showalter this bracelet because I think she'll like it."

"You've never given *me* a bracelet."

"If you want a bracelet, I will give you a bracelet."

"Yes, if that's what girls like Sandy wear, I want one."

"Look at Rama, wanting to go with the flow!"

We hang out inside the mean girls' restroom for four minutes before anyone enters. I pretend to fix my hair and Rama rearranges the folds of her scarf. By the time Sandy enters, I've primped for six minutes and am thoroughly sick of looking at myself. "Rama, isn't this bracelet cool?"

"Yeah."

"My older cousin, in New York, she says shoelace bracelets are the thing." I hold out the blue-and-white bracelet, hoping the bathroom fluorescence will make the silver threads gleam. "They are really easy to make, especially in Beatty Middle School colors."

"So pretty," Rama says with a lot of faux enthusiasm.

Sandy smiles. "That is nice. Can I see it?"

"Keep it. I can make more," I say. "I can teach you how to do—"

But Sandy beats it out of the restroom before I can say "it."

Only time will tell if my sad attempt at being nice made any difference in the world. Right now, it's clear that

161

Rama doesn't think it did because she's got her hand on her hip and she's shaking her head.

"Don't say anything."

"Do you know *anyone* in New York?"

"Nope."

"You still owe me a bracelet."

I'll make her a stupid bracelet this weekend. Right after the most beautiful sky scene of the year flies over my house. It happens tomorrow and she doesn't even know it's coming. My gift to her and it's something I can give without any parental unit fearing I'm messing with her culture. I may not know a boatful of facts like Wayne Kovok, but I know one thing. Everyone likes to stop and look at unusual things. Especially if they float over your house.

chapter 27

Here is a girl being shown the way by the universe.

Saturday before sunrise.

No one in the house is awake. Not even Larry.

When it is time, I go outside in the backyard. You can hear them coming by the sounds of hot air.

Shhhhh. Shhhhhh.

A sea of hot-air balloons sailing over our neighborhood. They come in this direction every year. They start at a park miles from here, and then float over rooftops all around town. They are like quiet surprises.

I look forward to this day like Christmas. It is one small thing in my life that has not changed.

I turn on my phone and call Rama.

"May I speak to Rama?"

"Do you have any eggs?"

"What?"

"Oh, I thought that was our secret phrase."

"Yeah, sure. Ha-ha! Eggs. I have something for you."

"A bracelet?"

"Better. Go out in your backyard and look at the sky."

"Is it falling?"

"Just go!"

I can hear her walking, door opening and closing. Then, "Wow! This is amazing."

"I know, right?"

I sit down on the dry grass and then lie flat next to the vegetables so that I can watch the balloons.

Shhhhhh. Shhhhh.

I love that sound.

One is striped like a rainbow. Another is the Lone Star flag. There is Darth Vader's head, which is always Dad's favorite. Also, a giant bumblebee, and I swear the guy in the basket waved at me. I wave back.

Shhhhhh.

There are at least fifty of them in the sky now, or so it seems. When they are silently floating and not pulling the lever to release hot air into the balloon, you can almost believe they aren't real things, but painted right onto the sky. Silently gliding. Peacefully sailing. Not in this world with problems, but above it where they are only concerned with air. Only traveling as fast as the wind blows.

"I think a guy waved at me," Rama says.

"Was it the bumblebee?"

"Yes!"

"Yeah, he waved at me, too."

I bet he could see Rama's scarf against the grass. She probably cuts a pretty image lying there.

Rama and I say nothing for a long while. Just watch the sky dotted with colors and advertisements and the breathy sound each time a balloon driver pushes hot air into the balloon.

"How long does this go on?" Rama asks.

"A good half hour."

"I wish I was up there."

"People would look small and insignificant."

"There would be no horrible Saturday math tutoring."

"Just clouds. And we could see where Woman Who Goes Somewhere is headed."

"Okay, I'm going to go now. I want my mom to see this."

I wish Mama and Laura would come out here, too, but they are both in their own worlds now. Sleeping or absorbing cartoons. And that is okay. Because there it is and I'm alone to see it.

My sign.

My sign to go forward is floating above. The Tom Thumb grocery store balloon. It almost makes me laugh out loud. A woman in the basket has a thick ponytail and a nice smile. We both wave at the same time. Woman Who Smiles scatters little bits of paper. They fall like white butterflies down onto Fargo Drive and beyond. I wait for one of them to come to me. A coupon.

Five dollars toward anything in the store. Today only.

The balloon hangs in the sky. I want to be in the basket and see the view from above. Thank the woman for the coupon. I bet life looks easy. Quiet. Safe.

And then the Tom Thumb descends slowly and looks to be barely above the rooftops. Slowly and gently, it falls toward Fargo Drive. It falls!

Now, it just seems to skim the trees. Something must be wrong. Really wrong. Will it land on our street or at the intersection? I can't believe it is going down, light as a feather.

My phone rings. "Are you watching this?"

"Yes, I see it coming down near your house. Do they seem to be okay?"

"It's falling slowly. No trees nearby," she says. "Wait, it's landing at the intersection, right in the center!"

I hang up and run to our front yard. A big, superwide

truck breezes down our street. It has a giant sign on the side of it that reads TOM THUMB CHASE VEHICLE. And then, from a distance I watch the billowy material of the balloon fall to the street softly, layer upon layer. And one last *shhhhh*.

If a balloon can land safely on Fargo Drive, then a girl can walk to the grocery store. Don't ask me why this makes so much sense. It just does.

This is my sign.

chapter 28

Here is a girl with a mission and a five-dollar-off-anything coupon. Good for today only!

I've thought it out. The conversation might go like this.

We don't have any other ideas except to ask the Jenningses for a ride, I will say. Mama hasn't wanted to ask for any help, which seems like backward thinking to me. The topic we don't speak of is all tangled up with her pride. The pamphlets about agoraphobia hidden in Mama's drawer indicate this is a common response.

Patients often want to try to beat this condition themselves and refuse help and treatment.

Let me think about it, Mama will say.

And I will respond, *Mama, I'm hungry!* and it will be this that makes her get out of her bed.

I step into her room.

"Mama, I'm going to the store," I tell her. She is rolled up under her comforter this morning, drinking coffee made of three-day-old grounds. She doesn't know my sneakers already walked 1.2 miles with me in them. She's going to freak out, but I'm prepared.

"Okay," she says. "Just take your phone."

"We really need dog food. And I could get you more coffee." I am already starting into my argument in favor of going alone on the long walk to the store when her response hits me.

"Okay," Mama says. "I'll get my purse."

Mama will get her purse.

Wait, Mama will get her purse?

That's it? No arguing? No debating? No *We can live on turnips, the original settlers didn't have a grocery store?*

I wasn't expecting this.

Mama gives me a look I don't recognize. A letting-me-go kind of look.

"Text me as soon as you get to the store," she says. "I'm also going to give you the Life Alert necklace, which you can push if you need help."

"If I've fallen and can't get up?"

"Well, the authorities will come if you push it, so——"

"The authorities aren't going to come. I'll be fine."

"Come and give me a hug."

Her arms surround me and I feel like I'm in a safe, warm circle. For a minute I don't want to leave this tiny safe space. Or our house. But there it is. A tiny voice. Or maybe it's the growl of a stomach. The gut instinct. Either way, it's the sound of urgency combined with the want of food. Mama didn't resist like I expected she would. I wonder if this is a good thing. Some other kind of sign. A sign of how change has come for Mama, too.

Here is a girl who will feel all the fear and go forward anyway.

I walk.

When I leave 4520 Fargo Drive, Woman Who Goes Somewhere is also stepping fast down our street. Since she is something of a pro at this walking thing, I pick up my pace to match hers. There is safety in pairs.

She is a mess, of course. Her hair spilling out from a pink baseball cap. Some large shopping bag slung over her shoulder. My hair is pulled back in a tight ninja-style ponytail. My backpack against my back. Change and dollars from Mama's purse float in my pocket. Change and dollars I will exchange for an actual gallon of milk and toilet paper and dog food and coffee.

The world seems at once too big and full of a thousand small details.

My skin is electric with fear. It's on high alert for danger and nefarious individuals.

Let's face it, I'm scared.

Very scared.

I'm trying to be courageous, five minutes at a time. Five more minutes. And then another five. Talking myself through it. Knowing I won't get lost as I've memorized the directions. I'm going to absorb every landmark and sign if it kills me.

Blocks of cement sidewalk along Fargo Drive mark my progress. Twelve squares. Check for nefarious people, creatures, and weather disruptions. Falling balloons and wannabe hipsters. Remember the rules about strangers and promises.

A stranger shouldn't promise you anything. It is a tactic to win you over.

Remember the rules about using your voice.

Your voice is your greatest weapon. Use it.

Remember the rules about screaming.

There are many.

At fifteen cement squares, I pass a little kid playing with a ball in his front yard. He is alone. No parental unit in sight and I want to protect him. Or shout a warning. Or dress him in orange.

More and more of Mama's rules spill out until it is crazy noisy inside my head. The only thing that breaks the spell is a sign against a fence.

BE AWARE OF DOG

I am aware. There is no one more aware than me.

Twenty-five squares and I've reached Bray Road. Bray Road is busy, four lanes across and a thirty-five-mile-per-hour speed limit. At Bray, Woman Who Goes Somewhere turns to the left and I go to the right. I walk along the sidewalk toward the intersection of Bray and Hooks Boulevard. I pass a jogger in a black top and dig my hands deep into my pockets. She nods. Nothing nefarious.

On the other side of Bray Road, there's a big empty gray-green field. It is for sale. I remember passing that real estate agent's sign when I was in the backseat of the green Toyota and Dad was driving me someplace, but I never stopped to notice his name. It's Wilson Carver, if you want to know. He has dark hair, great teeth, a wine-colored tie, and you can call him if interested in the twenty-five-thousand-square-foot lot for sale.

See you on the flip side, Mr. Carver.

I sight the crosswalk that separates me from store-bought food. It is a beacon. A few steps across and I will be away from a busy street full of fast cars shuttling strangers here and there. Strangers who shouldn't mess with me or they will be sorry. My screaming voice is legendary. At least, I hope that it is.

I step into the suburban shopping center and mentally draw a careful picture of the layout. Tom Thumb. Supercuts. Gas Station. Dry Cleaners. Jewelry Store.

Five minutes more. And it's not so bad.

There's also a row of clothing shops. The mannequins in one window wear colorful scarves and giant rings on fake fingers. It looks French to me. I'd like to stay and admire them awhile, but there's a slow-moving car behind me. I feel its heat like hot breath, hear the squeak of tires. If I turn, I'll see a scruffy face. Bearded. Reflective sunglasses. A gold tooth. Hook for one hand. A nefarious individual who captures young children.

Remember to never leave with a stranger. Scratch and claw and bite and kick with your legs, the strongest part of your body, but never leave with them if you want to be found again.

I picture myself doing all those things at once.

Here is a wild girl, scratching and clawing and surviving. Ka-pow!

Then there is a car right by my side and I sweat and boil like I'm a pot of water on a stove. I do my best to turn and look without it being obvious. When I do, it's just a slow-moving, blue-haired lady behind the wheel of a big blue car. Of all the people to worry about. Geesh!

Five minutes longer.

My heart beats faster. I identify a woman with a toddler pushing a stroller toward the Tom Thumb entrance.

Mothers with strollers are safe.

A group of teenagers crosses the parking lot and heads into the Supercuts store. They are laughing. Carefree. They have no worries. A haircut is a luxury no family who eats turnips can afford.

That should be the joke of the day. Except that it's true.

The electric doormat opens as Woman with Stroller enters Tom Thumb, me right behind her. The cool air sweeps me up and invites me inside.

I text Mama and she replies with a smiley face. I can picture her at the kitchen table. She will sit there staring at the salt and pepper shakers until I get back, her knuckles going white from gripping the table.

At the checkout, I place items on the conveyor belt. A sack of dog food as big as my backpack. Four apples. A four-pack of toilet paper. A half-gallon of milk. A small box of detergent. A pack of Wintergreen gum. And a package of M&Ms for Laura because she will not believe I walked here unless I return with a store-bought talisman.

I look at all my items and wonder if I can really carry them back to Fargo Drive without my arms snapping off.

Quick, I put the half-gallon of milk in the soda fridge right under the magazine stand. I would rather have clean-sheet day than fresh milk.

I stuff all that will fit into my backpack and carry the rest toward home inside white plastic bags. I regard Wilson Carver, still with his cardboard smile in the empty field. I count fourteen cars along Bray Road. I am aware of the dog on Fargo Drive. And I feel calm when I spot the same little boy, still playing with his ball in his front yard.

He, too, is miraculously safe on Fargo Drive. Or maybe it's no miracle. Maybe he's just not afraid.

The entire adventure took me an hour.

I put one shopping bag down at the door of 4520 Fargo Drive and unlock the door. I can't believe this is my hand, all etched with deep red grooves made from carrying grocery-filled Tom Thumb bags.

Here is the hand of Mysti Murphy, girl who buys food.

I display my store-bought trophies on the kitchen table. All of it except the gum. It is hiding in my pocket and it's for Rama.

"Oh…um…" Mama says nervously. "Are you okay? I mean. Oh, Mysti—"

"You don't even have to make a T-shirt with my face

on it because I am not missing," I say with as much sarcasm as I can muster.

"Well, I love you, so sue me."

Mama lowers herself into a kitchen chair and holds on to the side of the table. Her face says she is playing that scary movie inside her head called *Dangerous Things That Might Have Happened to My Daughter*. I put the apples away. Unwrap the toilet paper. Fill Larry's bowl with kibble.

Then I slice a fresh crisp apple and put three pieces in front of Mama. I promise you, fresh fruit tastes better if you bought it yourself.

"Why is Laura asleep?"

"She has a cold."

"I should make her some tea."

Mama sits at the table picking at the blue place mats while I heat up a mug of water in the microwave. She's gone to a far-off place, so I leave her there and bring the mug of tea to Laura.

"Knock, knock. Tea and M&Ms, dear sister."

"How was it? Scary?"

"A little. It's actually exhausting to be on alert for so many things."

"You look tired."

"Must be the reason Mama naps so much."

"Right."

"What does a dentist call his X-rays?"

"What?"

"Tooth pics," I tell her.

Not that I would know anything about a dentist firsthand.

chapter 29

Here is a girl missing her friend.

Wish I could talk to you.

☻

We need to do this project.

I gave you supplies.

A picture of the Alamo and Popsicle sticks?

Yeah.

Like I couldn't get that on my own.

I have basketball.

I have stuff too!

Just do it. It's easy.

Dork!

Dad?

Better, but not home yet.

R u still there?

Yeah. Don't know what 2 say.

Me neither.

Did you see that movie CREATURES?

Oh, yeah, I go to the movies all the time.

☺

chapter 30

Here is a girl who may have more hidden genius than she realizes.

It's a chilly morning. The sun is just barely breaking through the thick blanket of clouds. It's like it doesn't want to get up. I want to say, *Hey sun, I feel the same way, but we both have to get up.*

I make Mama fresh coffee because I went to the store two times over the weekend. (There's only so much you can fit into a backpack and you don't really want it to be obvious that you're carrying toilet paper.) We are stocked with baloney, tuna, macaroni and cheese in a box, and bananas. I swear to you that for as long as I live, I will never take a banana for granted again. Seriously. A banana will never go rotten on my watch.

So after the coffee gets going and Laura has had her breakfast, I manage to put my Texas History project into a supersized trash bag.

Mama calls down the hall.

"Bye, Mysti."

I wish she would get up and close the door behind me. She figures I will lock it myself, I guess.

Click.

I walk to the bus stop.

"What's that?" Rama's scarf is Aquamarine.

"School project. Sit next to me."

"Don't I always?"

"Well, yeah, but I need you to cover me so that this doesn't get messed up."

"Consider yourself covered."

RamaKhan!

Now I'm not saying I want to copycat Anibal Gomez and change my appearance and actions all at once, although I've been considering a makeover. I just figure that ever since that tree branch snapped, change has been forcing its way into my life. It's time to make friends with it. Do something on the outside that matches how I feel on the inside. For all I know, that is how Anibal decided to buy his first hat.

So as I was completing the Alamo project with those Popsicle sticks, old pieces of cardboard, and Mama's paints, I asked myself if anything about this assignment could reflect a girl who was embracing change.

When you ask yourself this kind of question, be prepared for an avalanche of possibilities.

It was a bit awkward carrying the project down to Ms. Overstreet's room before the homeroom bell rang, but I did it. Now, I sit in the homeroom class with a secret smile on my face (closed mouth, of course) because at least the project is finished and spectacularly original. No one will forget my Alamo.

I sit through announcements smiling.

Orange chicken with rice.

The girl batted away her memories of poultry humiliation and shame.

Who wants to enter the science contest? Grab a flier with all the details. There are great prizes this year!

The girl thought this was the school administration's subtle way of encouraging non-geeks to enter.

It's Bart Bartson's birthday today!

The girl thought poor Bart Bartson's parents lacked offspring-naming creativity on a rather colossal scale.

Math.

"Let's talk parallel lines today," Mr. Red announces. "I

don't know about you, but I see them everywhere. They're fascinating!"

The girl thought Mr. Red's exuberance over math was admirable, but not contagious.

Lunch.

At lunch I'm too nervous to eat. I chew on a stick of Wintergreen gum.

"Did you know gum is really just a form of synthetic rubber or polymer and was first sold in the 1860s?" Wayne asks.

"No, I didn't know that," I say. "How's the poetry block going?"

"Man, this poem we have to work out has a star in it. You know, when you wish upon a star, the star is already dead and your wish is really a few million light-years too late," Wayne says.

"You know, you are truly unforgettable, Wayne," I say.

"Thanks for the compliment."

"She doesn't mean unforgettable in the positive sense," Rama adds.

"I'm taking it in a positive way whether you meant it or not!" Wayne responds.

Texas History.

The quality of Alamo replicas in the classroom ranges

from "My dog could do that" to "Dude, I think your parents did that."

But not the Mysti *sans* Anibal project. *Sans* is French for "without."

On the outside, my project doesn't look like the Alamo at all. In fact, it looks curiously like the glass-and-metal pyramid that serves as the grand entrance to the Louvre Museum in Paris. It's not perfect. I think the dimensions are pretty good. The color is a pale Yellow Ochre painted over pizza-box cardboard. I superglued more than 100 black bobby pins all across the sides to replicate the 603 rhombus-shaped and 70 triangular glass segments of the actual pyramid. (If only Mr. Red was here to witness how much math I used in this project.) When the sun hits the metal, it actually looks cool.

"Um, Miss Murphy and Mr. Gomez, please come up to my desk and explain why there is a replica of the Louvre Museum in my Texas History classroom?" Ms. Overstreet asks.

I walk up to her desk. "There were once French settlers in Texas."

"Go on," Ms. Overstreet says.

And I do.

"It happened in 1685 under the command of King Louis the Fourteenth. The crew was supposed to set up a fort somewhere in Louisiana, but because of a navigational error, they landed in East Texas instead. Once they realized their error, they made the best of it," I say.

Anibal stands there with his hands in his pockets and his stupid mouth hanging open. Ms. Overstreet raps her fingers on her desk. Her diamond wedding ring is in the shape of the Lone Star State. Man, she found the one right guy to marry, I guess.

"When you have to do a project alone, you might as well do like the French and make the best of it. So I made something I'd like to have in my room," I reply.

"You realize that not doing the assignment in an appropriate manner will result in a bad grade," Ms. Overstreet states. "A zero. And that's for both of you."

Here is a girl who believed her Parisian emblem was perfect in all ways, both as a project and a reminder that smart girls can get back at dumb boys in interesting ways.

I take my seat.

The Louvre Museum model draws a crowd of admiration. I soak it up like the imaginary fancy French perfume that it is.

Parfait!

Sometimes doing the unexpected is the exact right thing to do.

When done with the proper amount of planning.

And hope.

I wait until the class is over and everyone walks out before I make my move.

"Is there something you want to talk about, Mysti?" Ms. Overstreet asks.

"*Oui*. That is French for 'yes,'" I say.

"I know it is."

Very carefully, I lift up the pyramid-shaped model. *Voilà*, there is my project underneath.

"Just so you know, I remembered the Alamo, Ms. Overstreet."

"So I see," she replies in surprise. "And why did you disguise one of the Lone Star State's greatest historical sites?"

"I didn't want my so-called partner to see this. It's sort of a joke."

"Your education is not a joke, Mysti."

"I know. It won't happen again."

"I'm still not certain you did the assignment correctly," she says. "I'll have to think about this."

I put the Louvre back on top of the Alamo. It's a perfect fit.

The bus line.

After school, the cheer squad paints posters outside near the bus line. So Anibal and his henchmen throw paper into my hair. I bite the inside of my mouth to keep from saying anything.

"Do you have birds living in that nest?" one of Anibal's henchmen says.

That is their biggest cut-down to me. About my hair. They are utterly unoriginal. I use my voice, my greatest weapon after all, and pretend I'm Girl Who Draws Tortoises as I shout, "Yes, Angry Birds! Get away!"

"Weirdo!"

So I walk home with Rama in the cool afternoon. "You are weird," she says.

I don't mind it coming from her.

"I'll take that as a compliment."

"That's sort of how I meant it."

By Mysti Murphy standards, the day was pretty great. Of course, I don't know if I will get a decent grade in Texas History, but I'm sure it won't be a zero. The main thing is that Anibal Gomez thinks he got a zero right now.

Zing! Don't mess with Mysti!

Rama even applauded me for getting back at Anibal in an intellectual way.

Zing!

And then, the walk home was crisp and cool and problem-free.

Double zing!

But that's the thing about life.

You sort of get one area of your life zinging along and then you have to look at those other areas that aren't so smooth.

Because I'd completely forgotten that Halloween is this week. Tomorrow, in fact. Tomorrow is Halloween.

According to our calendar, magical things are supposed to happen tomorrow. Magical things that will cure Dad's head and put 4520 Fargo Drive back at square one. Food. Shopping. Groceries. Ice cream. Long pants. Riding in the green Toyota. And Mama out of her Cold Midnight Blue guess-how-I'm-feeling-today funk.

According to our calendar, this was going to happen.

According to our calendar.

chapter 31

Here is a girl being introduced to Dad: The Sequel.

I am sitting at our kitchen table explaining life to
Laura. Judging by the confusion on her face, I might be
here until the sun sets. I mean, the hugging salt and pepper shakers seem to understand better than her.

"Dad still has a lot of recovery," I say.

"What does that mean?"

"He's not coming home."

"But I don't get it. He's awake, right?"

Since I knew Mama wouldn't tell me the truth, I got
on the kitchen phone and listened in earlier when she'd
talked to Dr. Randolph.

"It won't be back to normal so soon, Mrs. Murphy,"

Dr. Randolph said. "This part of the process is what we call emerging."

"What do you mean?"

"Well, your husband's memory is impaired. His muscle and motor skills will need to be rehabilitated. Recovery takes time. I know you get tired of me saying we should wait and see, but that's exactly what we should do."

Dr. Randolph went on with lots of medical talk. Dad is doing better, but things will not be back to normal anytime soon. In fact, Dad will not be home soon. Not tomorrow. Not any specific day. Dr. Randolph says we should do two things: Visit Dad and be patient with his progress.

I am still thinking about what this means when Laura punches my shoulder and says, "So, what did the doctor say?"

"He said people just don't roll out of comas, come home, do the grocery shopping, and wash their cars in the driveway."

"So he's not coming home?"

"Not anytime soon from what I can tell. So be nice to Mama and stop leaving your socks all over the place."

"I'm always nice. Stop bossing me."

"Extra nice," I say. "Here she comes."

"What are you girls doing?" Mama asks.

"Just hanging out," I say.

"Does your hanging out include helping me with dinner?"

Helping her with dinner? I want to say that she would be helping me with dinner. That dinners by Mama are hard to come by. But I say nothing.

Here is how we make dinner.

I boil water for macaroni and cheese, then open a can of tuna fish to mix in.

Mama slices two apples.

Laura puts three plates on the kitchen table and folds the napkins in perfect triangles.

Laura and Mama sit at the table while I do all the rest.

That is how *we* make dinner.

But when Mama sits down to eat, she looks tired to the bone. She's so tired she stares at the salt and pepper shakers at the center of the table and says, "Well, I don't know why I thought someone in a coma would just roll out of bed and drive home. How stupid could I be?"

"That's not stupid, Mama," Laura says. "None of us have experience with comas."

"I mean, I really thought it was like he would be gone

for an eight-week trip or something." Mama nervously laughs. "And now, well. I'm grateful for all this, but..."

She trails off and looks across the family room at nothing in particular.

I already knew this day was coming. A calendar on the wall, counting off the days until you thought "normal" would walk back through the door, doesn't really mean anything. I want to tell her that all those red checks were just red checks of hope. Not red checks of certainty. She can count on me now. I will walk in and out the door of 4520 Fargo Drive and get the things we need. I will do that and more. But I don't get a chance to say this because I don't take the chance. At least, I wait until the last minute to say anything and then Mama starts down the hall. By the time I decide to get up from the table, she has closed her door softly. The click close of her door makes a two-syllable sound.

Not now.

So I clean up the kitchen and stomp a bunch of ants on the floor. They got past the chalk line somehow. Then I go to my room and make myself fall asleep reading Dad's old copy of *The Old Man and the Sea* by Hemingway. I'd wedged this book out from under my bed and so my bed is now tilted. I need to find another book to help prop up the frame.

Before I know it, it is morning and it's time to go and see Dad. The night and day have just run together and we are outside.

Mr. Jennings has his car idling in front of our house. Next thing, we are standing in front of Dr. Randolph, who directs his attention at Laura because I guess she looks more scared than I do.

"It will be okay, sweetheart. Your father's speech is still a little slower than what you're used to. So be patient, okay? Just talk about some of your favorite things. Squeeze his hand. Speak in a calm voice. Got it?"

Dr. Randolph is super optimistic. I've come to like that about him. He doesn't focus on what's wrong, but what's possible. I'm going to tell Rama about him.

Speak.

Squeeze.

Listen.

We could do these things.

Laura and I enter his room. It smells all fresh and flowery. Dad is sitting up, a big pillow supporting his back. As soon as he sees us, his eyes fill with tears. There is a familiar Dad smile on his face. Laura throws herself onto him in an extreme hug. Dad runs his hand gently through her long brown hair. Then Laura runs her hand through his hair, too. It is starting to grow back in around the patch where they shaved it for surgery. "My girls." His voice sounds scratchy like an old man's voice.

"How are you?" he asks.

Laura is a dump truck of information. She talks all about herself, her drawings, her teachers, who she doesn't like at school, and who is bothering her at recess. Actually, I learn a few new things about her. That she'd won a school award for being nice to a new classmate. And that there was a mystery stink in the second-grade hallway that required the janitor to search every single locker and bring in huge fans to air everything out.

"It smelled so rotten that the teachers thought an animal had died, but it turned out that Ari Goldman just left a banana in his locker for an eternity," Laura says. "Ari Goldman is in love with me. The other boys told me he said this, but I don't love him back. I like Albert okay. Oh my gosh, did I tell you that Albert had his mother's underwear in his backpack? He said that he always puts his backpack in the laundry room and it must have just accidentally dropped in there. So embarrassing!"

"How are you, Mysti?" Dad asks when Laura finally stops reciting her autobiography.

"Fine." I sound like Mama. Faux.

"Mysti is doing everything at home, Dad. She gets the food, does the laundry, and got a zero on her class project." I pinch Laura's arm. Like Anibal Gomez, Laura doesn't know that I did two projects.

"It's all good, Dad. I didn't get a zero," I say.

"Proud of you," Dad says. He squeezes my hand and I squeeze his back. I hold back tears until I feel my head throb because I don't want to cry in front of him. And I know that my tears would be the pitiful cry of some mushy girl who forgot to worry about her dad and spent more time thinking up bracelet making and models of Paris museums. If I had any sense, I would pinch myself.

"Got any jokes?"

Oh man, this is going to be hard. Calling up a joke right when you'd just like to go find a bathroom stall and bawl for about five minutes.

Here is a girl summoning her superpowers.

"Do you know what you call unhappy cranberries? Blueberries."

That is the stupidest joke, but the only one I can think of on the spot.

"Really proud of you," Dad says again. I kiss his cheek and promise to call him every day. It is then I notice that he has a framed picture of me and Laura on his bedside table.

"From your mother," he says.

Back at home, there is evidence Mama has been in deep-cleaning mode. The air smells like glass cleaner and there are vacuum tracks on the carpet. This is what she does sometimes. She organizes the only thing she can, which is the house.

I go to the living room bookshelf and steal a framed picture of Dad. I carry it to my super-organized Mama-fied room and place it on my nightstand.

"What's up, Dad? You like being in here? Great."

Then I get Mama and Daddy's wedding album and study all the pages. The album is like looking at one of Laura's old picture books. A wordless story with a happy ending. There are my grandparents, who have since passed away. There is Dad standing outside a church. My grandmother putting a lace veil on Mama's head. Pink flowers. A picture of wedding rings on a pillow. A three-tiered cake dripping with orange and pink flowers. And finally, Mama and Dad kissing at the altar, preparing to live happily ever after.

I wonder if they knew change was coming for them.

I touch the picture of Mama. She is actually there in the church. She is in a place that is not 4520 Fargo Drive. There are no other pictures like this on the planet. None with Mama in a different background at all.

Man, I would really love to step inside these pages for a few minutes and hang out with my parents. See what it was like before the topic we don't speak of. Be in a time when she actually went someplace to buy a white dress and married a redheaded guy.

"What are you looking at?" Mama asks. I didn't even hear her step into the hallway. I'm glad the album is partially covered by my comforter.

"Just a book showing events in Texas history."

chapter 32

Here is a girl feeling the rumble and tremor of the universe.

Saturday morning and the ants are invading our kitchen like Santa Anna's army: by the thousands. I tell Laura to get the chalk from the garage and she goes to town drawing around the baseboards. Mama is still asleep, of course. Laura and I eat breakfast in front of the TV. The air is cool and full of fall. I open all the windows in the house. I decide that it should be clean-sheet day for everyone, so I run around like a wild maid until the house is filled with the scent of dryer sheets. I want to make everything just right so that when I come back from the store today, everything will be just right for my surprise. Today is the day I get my hair cut. I had a dream about it. In the dream, I had short hair and I was wearing a French beret. In the dream, I looked happy. When I woke up, I felt happy. Instead of waiting for change to happen, my new policy is to make it happen first.

In the afternoon, I tell Mama that I will be walking to the store again, did she want anything?

"I don't know."

I say, "Cookies. And Laura drank the last of the milk. And wouldn't this be a great day to make your fantastic banana bread?"

Okay, I'm buttering her up good for the surprise. I'm trying to get her to do something that makes her happy. Fresh bread. So what.

"Well, that does sound good. But I was thinking of ordering pizza tonight."

"Really? You will do that?"

"I'm trying, you know. I think I can take that small step," she says. Or maybe she is trying to not cook anymore. Who knows.

"Just wear the coat." She doesn't even look at me when she says this.

The coat.

The dreaded orange coat.

The one that magically turns a human into a walking safety cone. The one they can probably see from space. It is car-stopping, neon orange.

I want to say that it's not really that cold outside, why do I need a coat? Especially a hideous coat. But at least she is showing some signs of caring for my safety.

The price of freedom and cookies is the horrible, awful, fashion-offending orange coat. So I go.

I crash into Woman Who Goes Somewhere and believe it or not, she actually pauses.

Because I am *that* orange.

It must be said that with all her crazy outfits, mine is crazier.

I allow myself to become Aware of the Dog and only have one scary moment when I hear what sounds like a gunshot. Just so you know, a car running over a solid acorn makes a similar popping sound.

As I turn onto Bray Road, I seriously consider ditching the orange coat behind a bush. But if something happens to this coat, Mama will never let me out again even though, by some people's standards, the coat itself is nefarious.

I wave to Wilson Carver and his brilliant real-estate-agent smile.

Yeah, you dig this coat, don't you, Mr. Carver? What's that? You like my hair the way it is? Well, the thing is, you always have a good hair day on the day you decide to cut it. It's like the hair knows!

When I looked in the mirror this morning and brushed my hair, it looked super good. Sort of like the hair of a girl in high school. But the rest of me still looked tragically seventh grade. So now, as I walk past Wilson Carver and head toward the shopping strip, I'm even more excited about cutting it off. I've thought about it for a while. Maybe since the henchmen made their stupid threats. I lay in bed, stared at the Alamo, and listed ways I could take my own stand and stop gum from invading my hair.

Ponytail? Potentially easy to grab and target.

Baseball cap? Potentially stolen and flushed.

Haircut? Target destroyed. Potentially...hip?

Now as I cross the Tom Thumb parking lot, I think, *Here is a girl in love with the idea that her outside should match her inside. If a guy can change his world with a hat, a girl can change hers with a haircut.*

For the moment, I am a human safety cone from head to toe, standing in front of a giant Supercuts poster featuring a stranger with deep-red hair. The opposite of hip. But I take it as a sign that this is the haircut for me. Longer around the chin, short in the back. I will appear one way from the front, another from the back. It will confuse Beatty Middle School jerks and make it a challenge to lob things into the back of my head.

Inside the store, I sign my name on the sheet.

"Do you have an appointment?" a lady asks.

"No."

"Have a seat."

Soon, there are huge chunks of red hair on the floor. My old red hair.

"This style will really complement your features," Yvonne the stylist says.

This makes me feel solid about my decision to change my look. A genuine hairstylist believes in my choice and I feel so good I almost smile until I hear the stylist behind me tell an old gray-haired granny, "Oh, this style will really complement your features."

People can really let you down in unexpected places like Supercuts.

I get out of the chair. My head feels lighter. Around my feet, it looks like a red bear picked a spot to sit down and have a good shed. I step over it carefully.

Later, long hair.

My body tingles with excitement as I breeze through the Tom Thumb checkout with our groceries and those Halloween cookies with the orange frosting stuffed inside.

I float home with no long, heavy hair weighing me down. Even the grocery bags don't feel heavy today.

I pass the Jenningses' house and catch a whiff of a

strange chemical smell. Before you know it, I'm standing in the driveway, peering into the garage where the Next Great Thing is still being worked out.

Maybe I am curious.

Maybe I am delaying a possible lecture from Mama.

Maybe I have new-haircut regret.

"You might want to get away from here, ma'am," Mr. Jennings says. "Dangerous fumes."

"What caused them?" I ask.

"Powerful combinations."

"Are you closer to finishing it?"

"Let me just say that we've made an application to the national patent office," he says with a wink.

I move to leave just as Mr. Jennings calls out to me.

"I see Miss Murphy is reinventing herself with a new do."

My face turns hot and red.

"I heartily approve," he says. "Very elegant."

"Really?"

"Really."

I plunk the groceries on the kitchen counter and run to look in the mirror.

Here is a girl unsure of her decision.

"What happened to you?" Laura stands at my doorway, an appraising look in her eyes.

"Do you like it?"

With the slow careful movement of one of her favorite wildcats, Laura touches the back of my neck where the cut is "stacked." At least, that's what Yvonne of Supercuts called it.

"It feels good. Soft."

I put my hand on my neck. "Yes, but how does it look?"

"And we'll save lots of money on shampoo."

"You're not telling me the truth, are you?"

"Did you remember the cookies?"

"No cookies until you say what you think."

"I think it takes a lot of courage to wear this style."

I don't know about courage. It seemed like a good idea at the time. Now, it seems like Supercuts stylists should be trained to ask more questions before customers choose drastic hairdos.

Have you been under any stress lately? Are you lonely for your former best friend? Are you currently losing the "Notice Me, Sandy Showalter" challenge and deluded into thinking this tactic will work? If the answer to any of these questions is yes, you might want to consider a simple trim.

By dinnertime, I'd worked out that I should try to predict the rain of insults that will come at school. Because they no doubt will. Laura is the perfect person to perform this job.

"Okay, Laura, now I want you to think of the worst insult someone at school might say about my hair."

Laura takes her time, gives me a grand inspection.

"Any time you're ready."

"Don't rush creativity."

"Fine."

"I'm not going to say it out loud because you'll hit me."

"I will not. You are free to insult me without consequence."

Laura steals a piece of notebook paper and a pencil and scribbles an insult, then dashes out into the hallway like a coward.

What happened to you, Mysti, did you get two haircuts or something?

That's not so bad.

"Halloween Oreos await you on the countertop."

I go down the hallway and start to open Mama's door to get her reaction.

"Mysti, don't go in there," Laura shouts.

"Why not?"

"She's been crying and looking at her wedding album."

Didn't I put the wedding album back on the shelf? Or did I leave it out for all to see?

I open her door anyway.

"I'm back."

"Good girl," she says. "Please close the door tight, Mysti. I have a headache all of a sudden."

"Want to watch *Judge Judy* later?"

"Oh, yes."

Here is the joke I was going to tell:

What did one mountain say to the other mountain after the earthquake?

It's not my fault!

Mama stays in her room and there is no ordering of pizza or making banana bread. I close all the windows when it gets dark. Laura and I have cookies and milk for dinner because no one wants macaroni and tuna again.

It's Monday morning before school. Laura receives five dollars to lob more insults at me so that I can develop an insult callus big enough to shove me out the door. Laura tosses out verbal missiles that might have made a lesser girl wince.

Who do you think you're trying to be?

The fashion police will be ticketing you later!

Did you run into the back of some garden shears?

Did you let your dog cut your hair?

Now appearing: Mis-take Murphy.

Ooh, that last one stings. (I wonder how Anibal Gomez and his henchmen have failed to come up with Mis-take on their own.)

Laura suggests I wear as much black as possible.

"Your hair now has an edge. You should dress with an edge, too, so it looks like you did this on purpose," she says.

"I did do it on purpose!"

"Here is a black shirt I stole from Mama's closet," she says. "Here is a slap-band bracelet I made for you with a black marker." The bracelet smells pungent with ink. I give myself one more quick glance in the mirror. What shines back is not a fashion model, but not altogether unappealing, either.

Here is a girl regarding herself in the mirror and hoping that a complete stranger might perceive slight attractiveness in her ginger hair.

We pack up our lunches (bread and peanut butter and a protein bar) and head toward the front door.

"Bye, girls," Mama says as she heads for the kitchen. "Have a good day."

"Bye, Mama."

"Thanks for getting the lunches together and everything," Mama says.

No comments from her about my hair.

She must hate it. Nothing I can do about that now.

At the bus stop.

I detect several glances at the bus stop and on the

ride to school. Rama does a double take and then gives me a thumbs-up as if she was in on my whole weekend makeover.

"Nice, Mysti," Rama says.

"Really?"

"Would I lie to you?"

"No. You would tell me if I looked like a lawn mower ran over me."

"I am nothing if not brutally honest," she says. "Which is why you like me so much."

"The brutality of your honesty is both your best and worst quality, depending on who it's aimed at."

"I'll take that as a compliment."

"I knew you would."

Morning.

Homeroom classmates try not to stare in an obvious way, but they lack the art of subtlety. Even *I* know how to give a sideways glance.

Lunchtime.

"It's really growing on me," Rama says. "Maybe I should do that to my hair."

"How would anyone know if you got a haircut?" I ask. "Would you ever show it to me?"

"It would be against my religion, remember? But maybe," she says, tugging at her scarf, which is a beautiful shade of Rosemarie Pink today. "Wait a minute, Mysti. She's coming."

"Who?"

Sandy Showalter stops at our lunch table. At the Loser Island.

"Your hair is pretty. Are you doing a whole French theme now or something?"

Sandy Showalter just paid me a compliment.

Wait, Sandy Showalter just paid me a compliment?

I wasn't prepared for this, so I just shrug.

Sandy smiles and moves back into her natural habitat.

"It's starting to happen," Rama says.

"What?"

"This is what they do. They will like you now. People like the new thing. The new thing is exciting until it's the old thing. Then, *poof*!"

"*Poof*?"

"I've seen it happen. Do you know what fickle means?"

"Of course I know what it means."

Here is a girl thinking the word fickle *is desperately underused in modern times.*

"You just wait and see. Be wary."

"Sandy's not bad."

"Just be very wary."

"Okay, I get it. I'm thoroughly wary."

"I'm still waiting for my bracelet, too."

"I'm still waiting for a lot of things."

Girl Who Likes Horses and Girl Who Draws Tortoises come by. In unison they say, "Nice hair."

I don't know exactly what Rama was predicting, but it gives me a little boost, I have to tell you.

Poof!

My hope grows.

In the hallways.

"About our Texas History Alamo project," Anibal Gomez says. "I heard about what you did, but we need to redo it."

"You're incredible."

He smiles like I complimented him. Boys do not always get when you are mocking them.

He says, "Thanks."

Texas History.

I play with Laura's bracelet all through Ms. Overstreet's discussion of important people in the Texas Revolution. There is a black marker stain around my wrist. When class is over and the bell rings, Ms. Overstreet corners me.

"Please stay for a minute, Mysti."

I stay.

She talks.

"You know, it's okay to want to experiment with your style, and sometimes, even your attitude toward education and assignments," Ms. Overstreet says. "But sometimes that is a sign."

"A sign?"

"That you're going through something weighty and serious."

"Ms. Overstreet, I'm going through seventh grade. It's very weighty and serious."

"Don't deflect with humor," Ms. Overstreet says. "This ain't my first rodeo."

I don't doubt one bit that Ms. Overstreet has attended many rodeos.

"May I go now?"

"My door is open." Actually, it's closed right now.

"I just have one question."

"You can ask me anything, Mysti."

"Why is it when a door is open it's ajar, but when a jar is open it's not adoor?"

In return for my observation, I receive the classic Ms. Overstreet head tilt to the side in mild annoyance with a side of grimace. I am not so dumb that I don't know what

Ms. Overstreet is getting at, so I say, "Thanks for asking." For this, I earn a smile.

I hope she understands that in the middle of a Texas History classroom, I feel more comfortable joking than discussing the weighty and serious issues of life. I mean, if we opened up that chapter, we might be up all night talking like mushy girls and Mr. Maynard, the janitor, would chase us out with his mop. And maybe, under different circumstances, I would stay and talk. If I didn't have to get home and see if I put Mama into a state of silent panic because of my haircut, I would wait to see if Ms. Overstreet would be up for an all-nighter. I really would.

chapter 33

Here is a girl standing at the intersection of I Miss Talking to You Street and You Annoy Me Drive.

I am in my room staring at the message alert on my phone.

Never have I been a person who looks at the name and thinks, should I answer this text? No, I answer everything and everyone. I am like the dogs in that Pavlov experiment Laura and I learned about on Animal Planet the other night. Every time Dr. Pavlov rang a bell, the dog would be given food. So the dog always went running toward the sound of a bell.

I am the Pavlov's dog of cell phones.

Bleep and here I come running.

Hey, M.

Hey.

Let's redo the project. K?

Nope.

Why not. It'll b fun!!

U didn't do it the first time.

Don't be trippin. I did 2. Don't be a jerk.

Me?

Yeah.

Call off the Sandy thing and I'll help.

UR jealous.

NO WAY.

UR annoying.

I look at my phone and don't respond. Soon, Anibal messages a string of question marks. I don't do anything. I don't want to be a dog who runs toward something just because a bell is ringing. I want to walk someplace far away from here. Maybe just to Tom Thumb to buy a loaf of French bread. I could eat it in front of the computer screen while I look at the Eiffel Tower cam. I would pretend I left my phone on the plane to Paris. *Oh, did you call? Sorry, I was dining with the French.*

chapter 34

Here is a girl noticing that she's been noticed.

It is the next day and it unfortunately has a lot in common with yesterday.

Laura won't stop insulting my haircut even though I told her that was a one-day deal. So now it is a marbles-under-the-sheets day for her.

Mama didn't say anything about my new style, but that's mainly because she stayed holed up in her room all afternoon and night and completed all her parenting duties by shouting from her bed.

"Hey, stop fighting and finish your homework. Hey, would someone unload the dishwasher? Hey, would someone bring in the mail?"

Hey, we'll get right to it.

So I got to school another day with no parental comments on my *coiffure*, which is French for "hairdo."

But things are looking up in the hallways of Beatty Middle School.

Rama Khan, Girl with Sap Lake Green Scarf, attacks my shoulder and pulls me out of the crowd on my way to the cafeteria. "Top secret information. Wayne overheard a conversation in the boys' bathroom."

"Alert the media. I hear girls talking in the bathroom all the time. Why do girls talk between the stalls anyway? That's weird."

"It involved Anibal Gomez and the henchmen. Anibal is ignoring you *on purpose.*"

Here is a girl musing that the activity of ignoring is almost never an accident.

"Well."

"Mysti, the henchmen are forcing him to do it in exchange for friendship and cool status. They're even all performing together in the talent show."

"They have talent?"

"Who knows. And don't make a joke. This is serious."

Maybe it is the crisp fall air that gives me the edge. Maybe it is my new hairdo from Yvonne at Supercuts. Maybe I can trust Rama Khan.

"I've known this all along, Dr. Khan."

"What?"

I've probably read a thousand and one books in my life. So I know this is the part of the story where someone like *moi* is supposed to take a deep breath that shows my profound relief that the truth is finally, *finally* going to come out. I've always thought those stories were fake. I've never once taken the deep breath of relief in front of another human being.

"I might as well tell you," I say, taking a deep breath. "Anibal told me he was going to ignore me at the beginning of the school year until he achieved hipster status and got Sandy Showalter's attention. Specifically, her phone number and a complimentary exchange of friendly texts." I realize how truly pathetic it sounds, which is why I've never told her before. Rama has come to a dead stop, hand on her hip, mouth open. Man, the sharpness of her look could slice a bagel.

"You agreed to this?"

"I was really just doing him a favor." Double pathetic.

"Mysti, you really are weird because—"

"Because even a sixth grader can see the problems of this situation? Tell me something I don't know. It's about to be over, anyway. The fall social was our deadline. Then it stops. You can get to know Anibal better then. Hey, look, it's Wacky Cake day!"

"Don't make a joke, Mysti. You always make a joke."

Of course I do. Joking is like having a superhero deflector shield for those times when you feel like a turtle without its shell. Has she forgotten how Wayne Kovok educated us on the life expectancy of turtles without shells? Maybe she wasn't listening that day. Seventh graders need deflectors like turtles need shells.

"Come on, Mysti."

Rama Khan is not amused and can really get past my shield with her tone of voice. That is the real and true reason I like her. She's not mushy. I will make her a bracelet today.

"On the walk home, I'll tell you everything. And bonus! I'll also say I agree with you that I'm pathetic, okay?"

"Will you also agree to be in the talent show?"

Now it is my turn to stop on a dime.

"Talent show? You need your head examined. You weren't here last year so I'll cut you some slack, but I am never doing that again."

"My mother wants me to enter and play the violin."

"Well, enter, then."

We sit down at the Loser Island and try to make eye contact with Wayne. But he's in a trance.

Those ribbons. Those blue-and-white ribbons.

They have shiny power that cannot be explained.

There is the entire cheer squad, bouncing their way through the lunch line. Looking every bit filled with spirit. They are together, minus one. Minus Sandy Showalter. I am now just as obsessed with spotting her in the lunchroom as Anibal Gomez is, and don't like this about myself one bit.

I whisper to Rama, "Let's mess with Wayne."

"Look, I have hummus in my lunch," Rama announces.

"Oh, PB and J for me," I say to her.

Still nothing from Wayne of the "Did you know" questions. You would think he'd have some fact at the ready about hummus.

"Did you know that girls *love* iambic pentameter?" I say. Wayne hates poetry.

"I don't get iambic pentameter," Wayne snaps. "I wasn't supposed to understand poetry!" He slams his book, which is ironically titled *Understanding Poetry*.

And then the universe messes with us.

There she is. Sandy Showalter. And she is next to an older version of Sandy Showalter. You know how you can look at a woman and know she was probably pretty once but now her beauty is all faded? That's how this woman looks. A little faded.

"What about over here?" older Sandy Showalter says, and I see she's pointing a shiny red-painted fingernail toward the Loser Island.

"Um, we can sit where I usually sit," Sandy offers.

But Sandy's too late. The woman has staked out a seat on the Island.

"Hello, everyone," older Sandy says. "How's everyone today? Are you all friends with my daughter, Sandy?" Sandy's mom smiles and it wakes up all her faded beauty. A good smile will do that.

"This is Mysti and that's Wayne," Sandy says to her mother. "I'm sorry, I don't know your name?"

"Rama," Rama says.

Wayne and I have a "See who can turn redder" contest and he wins by a mile. He picks up *Understanding Poetry* and tries to understand, only the book is upside down. He'll probably just think it's stupid poetry messing with him.

"Hi, Sandy," I say. "Hi, Sandy's mom."

"Mysti made this supercool project for Texas History," Sandy says. "The entrance to the Louvre Museum."

"I didn't know there was a Louvre in Texas," Sandy's mom replies.

"Mysti, I would *love* to have one of those. Maybe you could show me how. I'm totally into Paris."

I pinch off tiny bites of my PB and J and wonder why she is talking to me like I'm normal. This is slightly challenging to think about when someone with a Naples Yellow scarf is kicking you under the table.

"Sure, Sandy, that would be fun."

"Let's exchange numbers," she says.

Kick.

And I say, "Sure."

We exchange numbers. I have Sandy Showalter's number. Can the exchange of friendly texts be far away? No.

"Sandy tells me there's a social coming up," Sandy's mom says.

"Mom, don't embarrass me!" Sandy has perfected the art of the eye roll like no one I've seen.

It comes to me that I'm grateful for Mama's lack of driving. We can file this chapter under "Mama embarrassing me at school—Events that will never happen to Mysti Murphy."

Sandy eats her salad. Her fingernails are painted blue and white. There are tiny bear-paw prints made of glitter on her thumbs. I catch Wayne stealing glances at her fingernails. Everyone is silent except Sandy's mom.

Sandy's mom is what Dad would call a chatterbox. She has lots of information to share about Sandy and it just ping-pongs all over the Island. We learn things like, Sandy is a great dancer, has a little brother who just broke his arm, and they have to go to Costco this weekend to look at fake Christmas trees.

We eat in slow motion, except for Wayne. He is now almost catatonic. Old and young Showalters leave the table, Sandy giving one last wave and toss of her ribbons.

"They're gone now, Wayne. You can breathe."

He grabs his lunch bag and book and takes off.

"I'd say that was interesting," Rama says. "But be wary. You know how those people are."

"Rama, being wary is exhausting."

"Don't forget—after school you're telling me your whole pathetic story and admitting that I'm a superior form of friend."

"I didn't sign on for all that."

"It's going to happen. Trust me. You will see."

After school, we walk home and I do tell her everything. I try to stick with the facts. I tell her that Anibal and I still text and talk on the phone. I tell her that he expressed concern about Dad. I make him sound human. Make him sound the opposite of how he's acting, which takes some verbal gymnastics on my part. I have to use the words *sensitive* and *caring*, words that don't come out easily. I leave out how I'm afraid of how much he's really changed, in ways I can't even describe to myself. I leave out how she is right about one thing. She is probably a superior form of friend. I don't tell her that because it will increase the size of her already-confident head so much she'll have to let out her scarf.

"So you see, Rama," I conclude, "Anibal is not one hundred percent jerk. This situation is not unlike an iceberg." This is me, trying to outsmart the girl with two career plans by using a Wayne Kovok factoid I picked up two days ago.

"An iceberg?"

"About eighty-eight percent of your typical iceberg lurks below the water. So we only really see a fraction of it on the surface. You've only seen a fraction of Anibal Gomez."

There. I don't know much, but this worked out nicely.

"Good try using a Wayne fact. I already heard him say that."

"Well, it works. What's underneath a person is what really matters."

"Except that I don't think Anibal Gomez is deep. He is one hundred percent surface."

Of course, Rama has a point. But in a very few short minutes I will be texting Anibal, and then in a day, Anibal and Rama will have lunch together and the iceberg situation will melt.

chapter 35

Here is a girl on the receiving end of truths she doesn't want to acknowledge.

Done!

Huh?

Lunch.

I saw. So?

So?

So!!!!

I have SS number.

So!

I'm just one text away from winning!

Whatever.

Eat lunch w/me now? Meet my friend Rama?

No way, loser!

?? why not??

Never going to happen.

I turn off my phone. I feel sick. I don't even respond to the Sandy Showalter victory text waiting there for me. I sort of feel like I just collided with an iceberg. My first instinct is to call Rama. But I don't. I don't want her to put words to my hurt. She wouldn't be mean about it, I know, but those words would still cut.

chapter 36

Here is a girl who hopes no one witnessed how she crashed into her front door because she was reading and not looking.

Once upon a time, Anibal Gomez was treated horribly by two fifth-grade boys. They constantly called him a loser. They were twins, these boys. The Snyder twins. They had a reputation for acting like they were the only ones in the world. The only ones on the playground. Anything and everything was theirs for the taking. If you were in their way, too bad. If they didn't like what you were wearing, too bad. If they noticed you made a bad grade on your test, too bad. They'd shout all these things at the top of their lungs.

Get out of my way!
Who dresses you?
Man, you're dumb.
And they liked to call people losers.

Anibal Gomez was tormented by the Snyder twins. They stole his books. Ripped his papers. Started calling him Cannonball Nomez. They wrote *loser* on his locker. And it was then that he said to me, *Mysti, I will never call someone a loser, not even if it's factually correct, like if they lost a game or something.*

Thankfully, the Snyder twins went off to some other middle school and did not bring their bombastic words to Beatty Middle School.

That was then.

This is now.

Proof that people change. Right there in black and white. Calling me a loser.

I crash into our front door. I know better than to read texts while walking, but this is different. I rub the sore spot on my forehead, then unlock our front door. Larry runs up to me, tail all awag.

But the rest of the house is quiet.

Too quiet.

Laura isn't home yet because she somehow wrangled

an after-school playdate with Rebecca. Another sign that Mama is less interested in us. For all I know, she sent Laura to the store.

I tiptoe down the hallway and peek into Mama's room. "Mama?"

The sheets are a tangled mess. No shower water running. No Mama on the patio painting. No sign of Mama in the kitchen except a precisely folded dish towel.

"Mama?"

My heart races and I sink into worry. There aren't really more surprising things than an agoraphobic mother who's gone missing.

Here is a girl in a story where there's a shocking plot twist: The mother who never leaves the house has left.

"Mama? Are you here?"

I go to the backyard. Surely she is out picking vegetables.

"Mama?"

I look in closets. Nothing.

I go to the garage, where maybe she's alphabetizing the deep freeze.

"Mama?"

My heart pounds. I feel queasy. I really need my dad right now. A wave of missing him washes over me.

"In here, honey."

Mama is seated in the driver's seat of the green Toyota.

Wait, Mama is seated in the driver's seat of the green Toyota?

"Mama?"

"Yes."

"I was looking for you."

"Well, I'm here."

"Why?"

"Just thinking."

She opens the car door. "Do you have homework?"

"Yes."

"I'm going to make dinner."

"Why?"

"What do you mean? I always make dinner."

"No, not really, Mama. Not lately."

"I guess I haven't done a lot of things lately."

I could unfurl my brain and let her know all the things she hasn't done. The list is long.

Here is a girl practicing quiet restraint.

"Well, go and do your homework. Next time you go to the store, get chicken, okay? And fresh spinach, please."

"Sure." I walk to my room fast.

I do my stupid math homework and then go out the front door and just sit. You would think Mama would say something, good or bad, about my haircut. Anything at all. But there is nothing. Mama is consistently inconsistent lately so what did I expect? A cake?

But it's not her fault that Anibal is the Mayor of Disappointment Town. He is the true villain of my life story.

So I sit on our cold porch until Laura gets home because I really don't want to be inside. Not even to get the dreaded orange coat, which I could really use right now. The wind is picking up and it chills me to the bone and makes me miss my scarf of long hair. My stomach twists and I try to shake it off and focus on good things, like how Sandy Showalter has my number and is also a fan of the French. And how Rama is really turning on her *RamaKhan* powers and being a friend who is encouraging me to be wary.

"What are you doing out here?" Laura asks as she hops up the steps.

That kid still has a lot of hop in her. I wish that didn't go away when you were twelve.

"Thinking."

"Do you want to think by yourself or do you want companionship?"

"You can stay, it's fine."

"What's wrong?"

"Mama. She's making dinner."

"Hoo-*ray*! I'm sick of macaroni, no offense."

Later, all three of us sit at the table and eat tuna fish with macaroni and cheese again. (Ingredients brought to you by Mysti Murphy, thank you very little.)

We wash the dishes together while Laura folds clothes. And Mama touches my hair, just a big chunk of it that frames my face. Her hand leaves a clump of sparkly soap bubbles on the ends.

"I like this," Mama says. "Very chic."

"I didn't think you'd noticed."

"I notice everything, Mysti. That's the problem."

"I don't understand."

It never occurred to me that noticing could lead to a problem like the topic we never speak of. It makes me want to go dig out a pamphlet in Mama's nightstand and see what's in there about fear and noticing.

She stares out the kitchen window. "I'm just too sensitive, I guess. That's what your father would say."

"No, he would say, *Melly, get over this already, you've got to overcome this or you'll plant fear in your daughters.*"

Mama drops the plate she was rinsing. It clatters to the bottom of the sink. Well, I've done it now. I wanted someone to feel as bad as I do. I guess I got my stupid wish.

"You know what, I have a headache. Finish this up and go to bed."

"Yes, ma'am."

I, too, have a headache. The kind I get when I'm determined not to cry.

After you've upset a person and they walk away, you can still feel the cloud of upset in the room. Like a bad smell, it takes some time to fade away. That's how it is for me now.

Here is a girl unable to make the kitchen completely clean.

chapter 37

Here is a girl in need of an honest chat.

Hello, RamaKhan.

Hey, MM.

Mmmmmmmm.

☺

Question.

Answer.

Do u ever feel like the world is showing you things you don't want to see?

Duh.

That's deep.

I wear scarves. World looks diff with scarf.

We'll go to Paris and we'll both wear scarves.

Good idea.

Good night, friend.

RamaKhan 4 ever

chapter 38

Here is a girl at risk of falling over because she has one foot in her backyard and one foot in the world.

Well, at least Mama has noticed that Laura is sick. Pale as chalk, rolled up on the couch, washcloth-on-her-head sick.

Animal Planet is on, of course, but she's not watching it. Mama sits on the floor, hair all pulled back in her orange scarf, stroking Laura's arm.

"What's going on?"

"She has a fever," Mama says. "We're out of Tylenol. But it is about to rain." The look in her eyes says it all. *I need you.* I like that look. I might even love it.

"I'll go get an umbrella," I tell her. "It's no problem."

"Take the Life Alert necklace. And the coat. And call me when you get there."

"It's not cold enough for the coat." The dreaded orange coat is not coming out.

"Just do it for me."

"Fine."

"Don't look at anyone, memorize license plates, and cross the street if you see a feral animal."

Here is a girl realizing her mother slept through previous chapters of the story in which the heroine already journeyed to the store unscathed.

"Seriously, Mama!"

"It was on the news," she says. "Feral hogs."

"There are no feral hogs on our street."

Feral animals have never before been on our list of what to be wary of in the world. But who knows. The more things change, the more strange things you might see on Fargo Drive.

It didn't matter too much because her words feel good to me, as if she is coming out of her depressed funk and morphing back into safety Mama. Safety Mama is better than sleeping Mama.

"Spinach and chicken, too, right?"

"And some chicken soup and orange juice would be good for Laura."

"And cookies," Laura manages. "I want animal crackers."

That kid never turns away an opportunity for a treat.

The field on Bray Road looks like a wasteland.

Gray.

Spooky.

Nefarious.

You could imagine zombies rising up from that field, all with the same face. Wilson Carver, zombie real estate agent.

All down the street everything is going from green to brown in a snap, the trees shrugging their leaves all at once and the laundry-water-colored clouds starting to drizzle. It could be a painting.

I pull the hood up on the dreaded orange coat and push on to the intersection. Then, a loud thunderclap. Unusual for November. I'd be scared if I had time to worry about weather.

I know the route so well that before long, I am stepping into Tom Thumb and rolling a cart through the aisles like this is what every twelve-year-old with a chic Supercut and a bad coat does.

Oh yes, I did know Honeycrisp apples were on sale!

My cart fills up with a nice big container of chicken soup and a huge bag of oyster crackers because, well, they were right there next to the soup. Then, on to the other items on my list. Animal crackers. Tea and honey. Chicken. Spinach. Two bottles of Tylenol, just in case.

Oh yes, I do need this hairspray for my new hair.

At the checkout, the girl says, "If you add just ten more dollars to your order, you can get a free turkey." Her name tag says BLESSED.

"Is that really your name?"

"Yes, indeed," she responds. "I'm truly Blessed. Now, about that turkey?"

If they go back and view the security cameras in Tom Thumb, they will see a stupefied red-haired girl try to make a decision about a frozen turkey on a cold day in November all while Christmas music plays overhead.

Here is a girl being given the offer of free food and, finding no real argument against it, darting back into the depths of the store for a ten-dollar item.

"This isn't for you?" Blessed asks as she scans the box of French Roast Brown home hair color.

"My mom."

"Turkey to station five," Blessed the checker calls into a speaker. A guy bags the groceries and then deposits a giant frozen turkey with a yellow plastic handle on it into my cart.

"Can I help you to your car?" he wants to know.

"No thanks."

The thing with grocery stores and credit cards is that you don't realize how much you are buying with your eyes until you carry it with your arms. And then you start to wonder if you really should have accepted a free frozen turkey.

But I was really thinking about how nice it would be to eat this potentially delicious turkey with Dad. Last year, all we could afford was that little rubbery turkey-breast thing Mama cooked up in a loaf pan. (Of course, I have to wonder if this free turkey thing was available last year.)

"Are you going out?" a woman says. Apparently, I am blocking part of the exit. I bundle up the two bags of groceries, stuff another bag into my backpack, and grab the turkey by the handle.

I walk.

I am cold.

And wet.

I now know what it is like to trudge.

I trudge.

Just crossing the Tom Thumb parking lot makes my arms so sore they might snap off like drumsticks. Stupid free turkey. The rain falls in a steady, miserable drizzle. The hair around my face is all soaked and stuck to my face in odd places. Without a free hand to brush it away or pull my orange hood back up, I trudge more.

As I cross the Tom Thumb parking lot, I dream about a steaming cup of tea and honey and a nice view of Animal Planet. Then, the screech of tires. Superbright lights. A car horn.

"Can't you see?" a person shouts.

"Sorry, buddy," another responds.

A red van is about five inches from me.

"Hey, are you okay? Sorry. Boy, glad you were wearing that bright orange. That coat's a lifesaver, huh?"

I set the turkey down for a moment and readjust it in my hand.

The dreaded orange coat just saved my life.

Wait, the dreaded orange coat just saved my life?

No way.

"That's between me and you, turkey."

I continue toward Bray Road, trying to focus on each cement sidewalk square.

The rain comes faster but I don't care.

I could already smell the aroma of Mama's garden-grown herbs blended into the stuffed, buttery bird. I pictured our table set with the fine china we never use. The tablecloth with the printed blue flowers. And best of all,

Mama coming fully out of the funk that sends her to her bedroom and keeps her from washing her hair.

Because I really needed her to wash her hair.

Mysti, this is just what I needed! she will say.

Then Dad, calling from the hospital.

Oh, Mysti, you are my hero! Save some for me because I'm coming home!

Even Laura will look at me with those big blue eyes, and tell me she'd clean my room for a month because I'd made all her dinner dreams come true.

"My taste buds are alive again!"

Here is a girl who would soon bring a heretofore unknown peace unto 4520 Fargo Drive, the consequences of which would include finally getting much-needed orthodontia and a trip to the mall.

Even though I am cold and my arms might snap off from the weight of the turkey, I am smiling.

Happy.

Hopeful.

But when I pause at the crosswalk, a giant Ford truck rolls through a puddle and a tsunami of rainwater drenches me solid. If that wasn't bad enough, through the window I can see Anibal Gomez looking at me and laughing. Well, this is the cold moment that shakes me back into reality and out of a warm storied world. The world where I pretend I'm an author observing a twelve-year-old character who looks a lot like myself, gap-toothed expression and all, and is prone to unfortunate plot twists.

Like carrying frozen turkeys in the rain.

What are the chances his family would drive by at the same time I'm covered in orange and holding a turkey?

About the same as a hot-air balloon landing on our block, I guess.

Anibal is looking and laughing. Well, like I've always known, people like to stop and look at unusual things.

And I'm sure I look unusual.

At the house, I run in from the cold as fast as someone carrying a frozen turkey can run.

Mama gives Laura the medicine and then brings me a clean, dry towel that she had warmed in the dryer. Man, she gets me sometimes. She hugs it around my back.

"Mysti."

That was all she said. Just my name.

Here is a girl hearing her name spoken with a certain quality not unlike an adjective.

"They were giving away free turkeys."

Mama regarded the turkey, almost caressing it.

"Oh, won't this be nice," she says. "I can't imagine how heavy this must have been in the rain."

"Nice for when Dad comes home at Thanksgiving, right? A real turkey."

I should have left well enough alone because the mention of him makes her go into cleaning mode.

"Yes," she says, wiping down the counter.

"And this is for you. That gray line on your head must disappear before Dad comes back." Mama holds the box of French Roast Brown home hair color. You would think I'd just given her the *Mona Lisa*.

"Mysti, well, that is so sweet of you. I must look a fright." Mama runs a hand through her hair.

I change my clothes and settle down to watch *What Animals Think, Part 2*. Maybe I will get insight into Larry's thoughts.

"I hope you feel better, Laura," I say to her.

"If I die, you must solve the mystery of the Woman. I saw her today and she was wearing a man's clothes and a ski hat."

"You aren't dying. You just have a fever."

"Just promise."

That kid is stubborn in sickness and in health.

"Okay, I promise," I say. "Hey, I got a giant turkey."

"I need a cup of water."

Laura already has a cup of water, but she wants me to play the part of dedicated sister so I bow to her commands.

She is too engrossed by the TV animals to be impressed about what I will now forever refer to as my poultry trophy, anyway.

She drinks her water and then her eyelids grow heavy. Before she goes to sleep, I tell her the joke of the day.

What did the dog say when he sat on the sandpaper?
Rough! Rough!

"Don't forget your promise. I must know the answer before my death."

"You should be in the talent show, Laura."

And then, there is a text from you-know-who.

I didn't know an orange had legs! 😊

Very funny.

Was to me.

What's up?

Not much. Just waitin 2 go 2 movies.

Oh.

I think your pic will make a nice poster!

No way!

Way!

Don't Anibal!

LOL!

Seriously! Just stop it.

Got 2 go.

Don't be a jerk!

Whatever. Nerd.

I open the stupid box of stupid animal crackers and eat them in front of the TV. I bite their legs off one at a time to make them suffer. That's how angry I feel right now. Take that, you stupid animal cracker.

It doesn't make me feel better. Just thirsty.

chapter 39

Here is a girl imagining that different fears have different weights.

Here's the thing about fears. We are only born with two.

The fear of falling.

The fear of loud noises.

All other fears are learned.

That is what it said in Mama's hidden pamphlets.

The purpose of these fears is to alert you to danger. All other fears can be unlearned. Therefore, it is important to monitor one's thought life and discern between negative and positive thoughts. Keep a journal and identify your fears. Then, identify the emotions that go along with them.

At school, I'm standing in front of my locker trying to decide what I'm most afraid of. I'm identifying the emotions that accompany my present fear. Because there is an eight-by-ten-inch picture on my locker featuring a dripping wet skinny girl in a ridiculously puffy orange coat holding a large frozen object. She looks like a wet orange duck. And as I glance around the hallways, I see copies of this picture. Everywhere.

Girl Who Wins Fashion-Disaster Prize.

The picture is pretty funny. I mean, I would laugh if it wasn't me. Kids pass me in the hallway and I hear the laughter and little comments. And really, that doesn't bother me. I hear comments all the time. So, if I'm going to do what the pamphlets say, I have to be honest.

My fear really isn't about the bad fashion statement.

My fear isn't that there are unknown copies of this picture in the world.

My fear isn't that some of the pictures already have cartoon captions on them.

My fear is that I've lost a friend forever.

My fear is that maybe he wasn't my friend all along.

I tear the picture off my locker and stuff it in my backpack.

I tell myself that nothing about this situation will block my greatest goal: getting to Paris. This is a picture like those in Mama's wedding album. This will be a picture of someone who will no longer exist in ten years.

But knowing that doesn't make my chest feel any lighter. In fact, my chest feels like an elephant sat on it.

Here comes Rama, waving one of the puffy-orange-coat pictures. Today, she is wearing a red scarf. Burgundy Wine.

"This is the work of that horrid Gomez boy!"

"I know."

"What are we going to do?"

"I guess you just won't save him from cancer."

"You've got that right."

"Why were you out walking in the rain like that anyway?"

"My sister needed medicine. She's sick."

"I'm sorry, Mysti. She'll be okay."

"How do you know?"

"Most everyone can be saved. It's a statistical probability."

Lunch.

We open sticks of Wintergreen gum. And then Wayne Kovok sits down at our table and reads, of course. And you will never guess, but the book is that thick one about

Steve Jobs's life that Mr. Jennings raves about. And it gives me a little hope.

"Wayne?" I ask.

"What?" Wayne mumbles.

"No fact *du jour*?"

"What? No. Too busy reading."

"That's the book my neighbor was reading."

"Yes, this guy Steve Jobs was incredible. He played all kinds of tricks on kids at school. He figured out how to make long-distance calls free and sold these boxes to people so that they could steal calls, too, and then when he was in college—"

"Wayne!" I have to stop him. He is a run-on sentence with a mouth. "So you are excited about it, that's good."

"I'm tired of being hassled by Joe Busby," Wayne remarks out of nowhere. "He doesn't believe I talked to this guy in China on my ham radio, but I did."

"Joe Busby is a jerk," I say. Joe Busby likes to tell everyone he is a model because he did some shirt ads for JC Penney and now owns a lifetime supply of plaid buttondowns. I call him Boy Who Lacks Humility.

"Okay then, you can be part of our club," Rama says.

"I don't want to be in a stupid girls' club," Wayne replies. "I just want to eat my sandwich."

"She's kidding, Wayne," I say. "And in case you hadn't noticed, you are already in our club."

"Did you know that Wayne is the most common middle name of criminals and serial killers?" Wayne says.

Here is a girl witnessing a potential inventor struggling mightily to emerge from poor Mr. Kovok's mind.

"I wouldn't say that to girls," I say.

"Don't worry, I find girls more complex than technology."

Wayne Kovok might have continued to forcibly educate us on circuits if Rama hadn't offered him a piece of Wintergreen gum so that he had to pause.

"Mysti, that poster was stupid," Wayne says.

"I've already forgotten about it," I say. "It was very juvenile."

Before we leave the cafeteria, Wayne turns to us and asks, "Are you guys going to the fall social?"

"Are you kidding?" I say. "No way."

"Girls make no sense. You tell me I'm in your club and then you do ... whatever," he says.

I feel bad for Wayne.

"Told you," Rama says.

"Told me what?"

"Told you he wanted to go," she says. "We can't go if you don't."

"Your mother wouldn't let you go anyway."

"I negotiated a summer math course for two hours at the social. As long as you go, of course."

"Are you sure you're not going to be an attorney? You do a lot of negotiating," I say.

"I can't go if you don't go. That was part of the negotiation. That, and I must be in the talent show. And I must win."

"You must?"

"My mother would be disappointed."

"Oh."

"And if I don't win, I'll be so despondent and will need someone to go to the social with me."

"Fine, I'll think about it," I say, just to get her off my back. Who wants to think about a fall social when she is currently the social joke of the day?

"Think of Wayne."

I think of Wayne.

You have to wonder if the Wayne Kovok of the future will become even more socially awkward and then invent the next big thing in his garage, the way Steve Jobs had done. Or live up to his name and become a serial killer. I hope for the first option and keep my head down the rest of the day.

Here is a girl who could foresee a future where Wayne Kovok confessed to becoming a criminal because no one would go to the seventh-grade fall social with him.

Texas History.

All I do is keep checking the clock.

Ms. Overstreet passes out a quiz about Texas revolutionary figures. She roams the aisles of the classroom and I can't help but be distracted by her golden belt buckle. It is, of course, in the shape of Texas and has two sparkly eyeballs embedded in it. Underneath them are the words THE EYES OF TEXAS.

I probably bomb the quiz completely, my head is so fizzy with worry. My education is crumbling around me like the stones of the Alamo because of illness and bad texts.

Then I hear the familiar refrain.

"Mysti, please wait a moment after class."

I wait.

She waits.

Everyone files out to go on with their Friday-night lives that probably include watching movies, eating popcorn, and not worrying about sick sisters and perfectly good green Toyotas that don't go anywhere.

"You don't seem like yourself," Ms. Overstreet says. "Is there anything I can help with?"

"Do you have a car?" I don't know why I said that because of course she has a car.

"Well, yes."

"You probably aren't allowed to drive a student to the hospital, though," I say.

"Are you sick?"

That is such a funny question I almost laugh.

The truth rises up from my feet and spills over my lips.

I tell her, "Mama never leaves the house."

There it is, in the middle of Texas History class. The short, sad biography of Mysti Murphy. All the important things you'd need to know about my life in five words.

"I mean, it's nothing," I say. "My sister's sick, but she's probably better now."

"Do you want to talk to Ms. Peet?"

Do I want Ms. Peet to talk at me, you mean? No, I don't.

"No, I just have to figure some things out."

"Well, I saw the poster today. I was going to mention that. Wish I'd caught the responsible party."

I get up from the desk. "It's okay. It was a little funny anyway."

By the time I get to the door, Ms. Overstreet stands abruptly and calls out, "Mysti! Don't forget what Sam Houston said. 'Do right and risk the consequences'!"

"He was scared, right?"

"Of course! Fear plus courage equals Texas hero!"

Ms. Overstreet is funny. Despite her attempts to be a guidance counselor to girls who growl in her class, she never for a moment stops believing in Texas heroism.

I hope it's contagious.

chapter 40

Here is a girl risking the consequences.

"People will come from all over the world to get an appointment with me so I need to start learning different languages, don't you think?" Rama asks as we walk home. "It's the least I can do. Maybe you and I can learn French together! Wouldn't that be great? And the waiting area will have beautiful carpets and a candy dispenser with Wintergreen gum and copies of *The Big Book of Facts* by Wayne Kovok. I will still go to lunch with you if you call far enough in advance, because my services will be in high demand, okay?"

"Okay."

Rama Khan. She is a dreamer. A dreamer with actual wings disguised as a scarf. Wings in fabric of every color.

I couldn't wait to get home and hear Laura's clear, well voice. I went through the front door of 4520 Fargo Drive and found her asleep on the couch.

"Is she better?"

"Much!" Mama says. Her face looks tired and old and smudged with Lemon Yellow oil paint.

"How was your day?" she asks.

"Fine."

Isn't that the word that doesn't really mean fine? Isn't that the word you use when you don't really want to talk about your day? When you just want someone to already know you are not fine?

Mama takes my hand and guides me to the kitchen table. I hope she is about to feed me bread or something. I could eat and go pull up my comforter and let it do what it's supposed to do. Comfort.

But there it is.

"It's you," Mama says, pleased as punch. "I worked all day on it."

There on the table next to the stupid hugging salt and pepper shakers is a painting of the Eiffel Tower, all done in sharp black paint against a bright white canvas. At the base of the tower is a red-haired girl with a chic haircut and a yellow dress.

The faux me is smiling.

The real me is not.

But Mama seems happy so I don't want to throw a rock through her fragile imaginary window of being fine.

But sometimes it's exhausting trying to keep someone happy, trying to keep worries away from them. You have to shut off your own feelings and concentrate on making them feel better, which haven't I been doing all this time? Pushing crackers under her door. Walking in the rain. Taking care of Laura. When is it my turn to feel bad out in the open instead of just making it clean-sheet day?

My mouth stays shut, but I can't keep that long, warm tear from rolling down my face. And darn it, I'm being a mushy girl, but who is here to see it.

"What is it?" she wants to know.

I can feel a big dark thing rising up from the bottom of my feet. A tremor not unlike what animals feel before an earthquake. It tells them to run. Escape. Get away from danger. But since there's no place to run, no higher ground of safety in 4520 Fargo Drive, all I can do is use my voice.

It's a scream.

My scream.

A loud and close and from-the-bottom-of-my-feet scream.

Your voice is your most powerful weapon.

I scream loud and long and Dad probably hears it at the hospital. It probably makes the crack in my ceiling grow wider. Makes a layer of dust fall off our green Toyota.

Maybe it was only loud inside my head.

Now it is a deafening quiet.

Laura doesn't even stir.

So I think I imagined the scream and kept it inside. I feel a headache bloom. And before you know it, I am really and truly leaving the area of danger the way animals do because all I want to do is smash the happy hugging salt and pepper shakers to bits. For their own safety, I must get out of here.

"Mysti, what's wrong?" Mama asks as I start toward the front door.

"That picture! That picture is *not* me!"

"What?"

"It's not me!"

"It's a picture, of course, but—"

"Never mind."

"But Mysti, I thought you loved Paris."

"I said never mind. Don't worry about it. Whatever. I'm going for a walk."

"But—"

"I'm fine."

Here is a girl who cannot control photos or paintings, but who might possibly solve a mystery.

I don't expect that Woman Who Goes Somewhere is particularly dangerous, but you never know.

She might be a secret spy, carrying messages to her contact, licensed to kill anyone in her path. She might be training for some kind of reality show where the winner gets a million dollars for doing the same thing the longest and if you get in the way of her and her prize, she will kick you into the next week.

Or she might just be garden-variety weird.

Probably.

The ground is damp and cold, even through the orange coat. Smoke rises up from two chimneys and the neighborhood smells like a fireplace.

Through the tree branches, I see someone coming down the sidewalk. Then I see the tail of a blue scarf and know it is Rama.

"Rama! Over here."

Rama sits down on the ground with me and I tell her my plan. "Thanks for coming over," I say.

"If she is a criminal, you'll have a witness and a medic," she says. "Plus, we can always act like we are goofy if she happens to notice us."

"We are goofy."

We wait.

We chew gum.

The clouds cover what little sunlight there is and I

worry that it will rain and make this walk miserable. More miserable.

"The social would be a night to remember."

"The *Titanic* sinking was also a night to remember."

"Come on, we should try."

"You have your optimism intact, Rama, and I like that about you. But if you think I'm going to embarrass myself even more at Beatty Middle School when I'm not required to be there, you are six shades of wrong. I'm just counting days off the calendar until it's over."

"Sad," Rama says. "Just sad."

Before I can protest more, Woman Who Goes Somewhere walks up wearing Cobalt Blue boots and Burnt Sienna pants. She is also wearing a short-sleeved Venetian Red T-shirt. Typical. She is never dressed for the right weather. At least that's one thing in the world you can count on. One thing.

I count to thirty and then Rama and I emerge from our hiding spot. We cross the street so that we aren't walking directly behind the Woman. The Woman's pace is slow. She walks to the end of Fargo Drive and turns left. Because I always turn right on my way to Tom Thumb, this is going to be new territory.

My heart beats a little faster when we make the left turn. The Woman stops for a second and adjusts her boot.

Rama and I pretend we are just out for a walk. Natural. I pause to tie my shoe. Only my shoes have Velcro straps so I have to act the part.

I check my watch. Eleven minutes have passed since we left 4520 Fargo Drive. Finally, Woman Who Goes Somewhere turns left down Boston Street.

We trail her to a house on Boston that features bright-blue shutters and an angel statue in the front yard. The Woman bends to pick up a morning paper and continues up the walk.

"Walk faster," I tell Rama, and we speed up on the opposite side of the street. As Woman Who Goes Somewhere unlocks the bright-blue front door, a big tabby cat darts out. That's when we hear her voice for the first time.

"Hello there, Lucy, let's go eat," she says to the cat, and walks inside the blue-door house. Her perky voice doesn't match her sloppy appearance. It's high and delicate. If she called you on the phone, you'd think, *Oh, this woman is nice and polite and her name is probably Amy.*

"What's our plan now?" Rama asks.

I must bring a good story back to Laura.

"I have to talk to her, ask her a question."

"What if she pulls that knife on you?"

"Nobody pulls a knife on people in broad daylight."

"It's not that bright out. This is the kind of weather most often described in books when something mysterious happens."

"This is you being helpful, right?"

"But as a future doctor of the world, I will know what to do if she uses her knife," Rama says. "I can make a tourniquet with my scarf."

"You would take that off for me?"

"Only if you were dying."

"That's sweet."

"Just don't get stabbed. My mother would be upset."

I should feel scared about approaching a stranger. A really strange stranger. Oh, Mama would be so upset. Too bad for her. I'm now more immune to suggestions of unusual danger. Perhaps that is not a good outcome of being a walker myself, but it is true. Abductions, feral animals, and strange people all seem to inhabit the television. You get used to being on alert.

We don't have to wait very long to make our next move. The wind shifts and you can feel a little rain in it. Rama and I pretend to be really interested in the acorns on the sidewalk. When Woman Who Goes Somewhere comes outside the house, she locks the door and walks farther down Boston.

We catch up to her.

"Hey."

The Woman turns. I don't spot a knife.

"What do you do in that house every day?"

"I feed the cat," Woman Who Might Be Called Amy says.

"That's it?"

"Yeah, the people had to go somewhere in a hurry," she replies. "Do I know you?"

"So you just walk around the neighborhood and go feed a stupid cat."

"That's what I said."

"Just walk by in mysterious clothes just for a stupid cat?" My voice cracks and I step closer to the Woman.

"Mysti, it's okay," Rama says.

"No, it's not. That's a stupid, stupid end to the story."

Woman Who Goes Somewhere looks confused. Slightly worried.

"Are you okay?" she asks.

"This is just ridiculous. Are you even from Texas?"

"Ohio, actually," the Woman says. "But I always thought I was meant to be a Texas girl."

Rama says, "It's okay, she was just curious. Have a nice day. *Au revoir.*"

This is Rama trying to make things nice. Smooth.

I pace around and kick the curb. "I can't believe it! I can't believe she was just feeding a stupid cat!"

"Calm down, Mysti!"

"Is there *no* mystery here? None at all? Nothing

is right. Couldn't I at least get a good story for my sister? I mean, I don't think I believe that woman. Feeding a cat. Really. She's dressing full-moon crazy, walking around, getting people's hopes up that something exciting is happening out in the world and it's all because of a stupid cat?"

"Mysti!"

"A cat!"

Laura will never believe me. It will make her sad to think that adventure and mystery didn't really walk past our house each day. That there is not something more exciting beyond our wood fence. Beyond our windows. Our front door. All the exciting things, when you get up close to them, are empty of excitement. Like oil paintings. They are copies, not the real thing. All that art is lying to you because guess what? The person who painted it did not actually *see* those flowers. Did not *see* those ships. Did not *see* a girl in Paris. The kids at school did not *see* the real me. They saw a cartoon picture that Anibal Gomez could use to get a few jokes.

It is all fake. Faux.

No one sees things clearly.

Everyone is too afraid to see things as they are.

"That was interesting," Rama says.

"Not interesting enough."

"I thought you were going to attack that woman. You were acting all…"

"Nefarious?"

"Yeah, nefarious. What's up with that?"

"I'm tired of being disappointed. Disappointment is exhausting."

We've reached my house. I don't want to go inside yet.

"Let's keep going," I say to Rama.

"You going to be okay?"

"Sure. Everything always turns out just okay. Maybe that's the problem. You want something different. Something more than okay. Okay is vanilla."

"That is why I like you. You want something more than the common seventh grader. That's why I sat next to you in the cafeteria."

"What? You sat next to me because there wasn't any place else to sit."

"No, I mean the second day."

"Oh."

"So dream for more. Dreams are free!"

"Are you getting all psychological on me now, Dr. Khan?"

"Psychology is my backup, backup plan."

"Don't give up on your plans, Rama. Really. Go and be a doctor who saves the world. If you don't, I couldn't take the disappointment. Go and do it. You are the bravest person I've ever met. There's hope for you."

We're in front of the green-shuttered house now. The house where a girl with lots of backup plans lives.

"You have hope, too. So forget the boy. Forget the cat."

"I can't believe it was just a cat!"

"Forget it!"

"I mean, a stupid cat! A cat that didn't even have an exotic name. Couldn't I get a Frisky McCracken or Onslow Von Paws or something? Is that too much to ask?"

"Mysti, your own dog is named Larry."

"RamaKhan!"

"RamaKhan!"

"Thanks, Girl with Scarf."

"No problem, Girl with a Great Friend."

That Rama. Sometimes she makes my heart dance.

chapter 41

Here is a girl helping her mother take secrets out of hearts and nightstand drawers.

I don't know how I came to be on the floor of my room, leaning into Larry with one arm, and wanting to sob like a tall two-year-old who didn't get what she wanted.

"Larry, isn't it funny that I've seen two pictures of myself today and this is the one that makes me mad? That is the joke of the day, right? I'm going to be known as Girl Who Carries Turkey, but this oil painting ticks me off!"

I tell Larry that it was just too unbearable to see a one-dimensional me in the place I most want to go in the world. Paris, where there is excitement and no one is ever bored. "Can you imagine, Larry, being bored in Paris? No, I'll be here on Fargo Drive forever. There are too many people to feed and make happy here anyway."

I flop back onto the carpet and stare hard at the widening zigzag crack in my ceiling and wish I could slip through it.

Here is a girl understanding that the crack is just trying to make room for her escape.

Then, a knock on the door.

"Go away," I shout through the door. "Go far away."

"I want to explain some things."

"Don't want to hear it right now, thank you." This is me trying to be nice and firm and calm. But I don't think my voice sounds nice and firm and calm.

"I need to explain that I have something called agoraphobia and—"

"Read the pamphlets. Already know that."

"Oh. You did?"

"Go away, please."

And then Mama makes a joke. Mama.

"Where would I go?" she asks. "How do you make an agoraphobic go far away?"

At first, I do not like that Mama makes me laugh through my anger. That emotion makes me uncomfortable. It is like she is burning up my right to be mad.

But I can't help but laugh.

A little.

Because you can't really tell an agoraphobic to go far away. That is a funny joke.

I open my door.

"I'm sorry," I say.

"I know," she says. "I understand."

She leans into my doorway so hard you can't tell if she is holding it up or it is holding her up. She and the house are part of each other.

"Then talk to the doctor and get help. What can I do to help? I'll ride with you in the car if that's what you want. Maybe we can duct-tape you to the seat or something."

Mama eases herself down to the floor of my room and attempts to smooth the carpet out, which is as impossible as it sounds.

"Mysti, I want you to understand something," she says. "You didn't break me and you cannot fix me."

"Who can fix you, then?"

Maybe Dad had been trying to fix her, too. Putting those pamphlets in the drawer.

"Who can fix you?" I ask again.

"You know, I do need to grow up," she says. "I do. I've let your dad do everything for me and it felt good and safe. Maybe that wasn't such a great idea."

"Thanks for the painting."

"It was silly."

"No, I like it," I say. "I just want it to be a real photograph, you know."

"Yes, I know," Mama says. "Someday, you'll send me that photograph and I can paint that, too, okay? Lots of photographs."

"Okay."

"Let's have some bread," Mama says. She goes to the kitchen for butter and plates. Her answer to everything. Fresh bread.

It is not such a terrible answer.

I have to step over Larry, who is presently lying across the kitchen floor.

Mama puts a plate and a piece of plain bread in front of me. We eat in silence until the rain starts to fall outside our house. The bread is good.

"You are old enough now to hear the story we don't speak of," Mama says. "It might help you understand. And the pamphlets say it's supposed to make me feel better each time I tell it."

"Does it?"

"I don't know," Mama says. "Here goes. The topic we never speak of spoken out loud."

You can feel the ground beneath our house tremble a

little more. As if the house knows. As if it's stretching out to make room for the truth.

Here is a girl listening to the rapidly unfurling story about the accident that shifted her mother's fears into high gear.

She was out to lunch with a coworker. He drove. She was the passenger. He told her a joke and she laughed so hard she doubled over. They didn't see the truck coming. Smash. Glass. Sirens. The smell of gasoline.

She cut her arm. They couldn't get her out.

For an hour.

And then everything was fine. Fine. And she went back to work the next day. But she stopped wanting to go out.

No, thank you, I can't go to your party.

And more and more staying home.

No, thank you, I won't be going.

Going to the grocery store one day, she had a panic attack, her first, right there in the produce section. Rapid breathing. Heart racing. Out of control and feeling like death was on its way.

She could never go back to that store.

Just the thought of going back to that place let the panic creep up her back.

And other places triggered it. Her greatest fear became

what could happen. A million things could happen. She'd do anything not to have a panic attack.

So there was a small square of town where she felt safe to drive. She drove that square. And then, one day, she couldn't cross a major street. Panic at the stoplight. Fear of making a left turn. Approaching any intersection and breaking out in a sweat and a pounding heart. To avoid this, she created maps that involved only right turns. This made running a ten-minute errand turn into a one-hour chore.

The square of safety got smaller. She got married and going places was less of a problem. Someone was there to help.

And the square of comfort became smaller again.

Until it was only 1400 square feet. 4520 Fargo Drive.

And she is sad and sorry.

The End.

We are silent as rocks now. She picks at the bread on her plate and for a moment I see her hand and her whole body, not as my mother, but as a woman out in the world.

Woman in a Car Accident.

"What happened to your coworker?" I ask.

"I married him," Mama says. "He was the funniest guy I ever met. And the most understanding."

"But he didn't get afraid after that crash."

"No."

Dad. Hasn't he always looked at life through different glasses?

I remember a time Dad heard a rattling sound in the car just after he'd taken it to be serviced. He got home and popped the hood up. Sure enough, there was a huge black wrench just sitting right there.

Mama said, "Oh my gosh, that wrench could have fallen into the engine while you were on the highway!"

Dad wiped it clean with a rag, placed it into his toolbox, and said, "Free wrench for me!" Two people never looked at one wrench with more opposite responses.

Just like that car wreck, I guess.

People are different.

That is not an Einsteinian observation, but once you get it, once it really sinks in, it seems profound. You sort of want to run out into the street and shout it. *Attention, attention! People are different! Do not expect them to be the same! If you do, your expectations may fall to earth like a balloon!*

Now, Mama tugs at her hair and twists it in her fingers and seems lost in her thoughts. She needs a good laugh.

"Joke of the day?"

"I love this part of the day. Yes!"

"How does a tiny man say good-bye?"

"How?"

"With a microwave."

We both laugh and accidentally knock heads and Larry turns up his head like we are crazy.

We both laugh when she says she's going to have to find a solution to the topic we just spoke of.

We both laugh when I tell her I'm plumb tired of turnips.

Then we go to her room and she takes out a pamphlet. She lets it rest on top of her nightstand, which is a start.

We lie on her bed and we watch Judge Judy tell a young man with a shiny purple tie that he better not lie because she is "like a truth machine."

"There are so many colors in your hair, Mysti. Red. Copper. Gold. Poppy."

"You always say that."

And I will always let her say that, too.

"Where is my story?" It is Laura, hands on her hips, all back to her healthy brat status.

"What?"

"You said you'd find out the truth about the Woman if I survived. Well, here I am. Alive!"

Because don't I know how much the truth can disappoint a girl, I make up a good story for Laura about the Woman.

A story. A story about how I thought it should be, not how it was.

Here is a girl who wishes more than anything that her own story would have an ending that, if not exactly Happily Ever After Yellow, would be some shade of hope.

It was as I told Laura a story that involved Woman Who Goes Somewhere and the witness protection program and feral cats that the idea came to me about a new story. Two words I tried without success to bat away as I got ready for bed. Two words that insisted on being present as I lay on my bed and looked out my window. Two words.

Talent show.

chapter 42

Here is a girl trying to change her story.

It was time. Sometimes you just know when it's time. Like when a former friend trips you in the hallway in front of his new friends.

"Nice trip, Missed-teeth," Anibal said.

I got to my feet slowly. Then I looked at Anibal. I looked for traces of the boy I knew. The boy who was smart and funny and slept on a broken water bed and even sometimes complained about how other people teased him about his weight.

That boy was nowhere in sight. That boy was a memory.

I made a list of all the possible options I had to fight back against Anibal, who was still working on changing my story. Still telling people I was a Girl with an Ugly Smile. Girl Who Dressed Funny. Well, none of my ideas to fight back against his meanness looked like storybook endings. Because characters in books are often aided by magic or miracles.

I had neither.

So I had to be in the talent show. Not because I have any new talent since last year. *Mais non*, which is French for "no."

No, not for that reason. I had to be in the talent show because kids were calling me those stupid names. It was really taking off across the seventh grade and the more Anibal did it, the more attention he got. I knew his names for me would stick until they came up with something else. That's what they do. Wayne Kovok was known as Boy with Palindrome Name until it was Dorkvok and then Boy Who Spews Facts. And Girl Who Likes Horses was always going to be just that. Rama was still pelted with cruel comments about her scarf. And in his own warped way, even Anibal Gomez was trying to shed being Boy Who Was Extra-Extra-Large Loser and become Boy Who Was a Hipster.

If I was ever going to get a name of my own choosing, I had to do something big and memorable enough to make kids forget the other names. And if one of the side effects of doing something big and memorable was showing Anibal Gomez that he hadn't won, well, fine. It was Ms. Overstreet who gave me the big and memorable idea the other day, even though she didn't realize it.

"Mysti Murphy, what do courageous Texans do when they encounter an almost insurmountable challenge?"

"They take a stand, Ms. Overstreet." This was what I could do in the talent show. Take a stand.

"A-plus, Miss Murphy!"

I wanted to tell her a lot of things. That she was easy to talk to. That it was nice to be able to tell one other person in the world about Mama. And mostly, that because of her, I would never forget the Alamo and was glad I had a small replica in my room. But I thought I'd get all mushy and cry so I just placed a gift on her desk. A sweet onion.

"The state vegetable of Texas!" Ms. Overstreet said. "I'm touched."

I'd practiced my "talent" for a couple of days in front of Mama and it made her cry. "These are good tears, Mysti," she'd said. "I'm so proud of you. You go do it!"

And it made Rama happy that I was going to do it, too. She even hugged me right before she went up onstage in a Sky Blue scarf, sat down, and played the violin so beautifully I thought she should give up her dreams to be a doctor. And even Wayne joined our stupid club and went onstage and performed a juggling routine that had the crowd clapping to the beat.

And then, me.

I walked up onstage feeling the hot fear race up my neck. I just floated. Principal Blakely stopped me and held up his clipboard. "Name and talent?"

"Mysti Murphy. A reading from the commandancy of the Alamo."

He looked over the rims of his wire-frame glasses. Like he was looking at a zoo exhibit. I nodded and he nodded. People do like to look at unusual things.

And I found myself at the center of the stage. Standing. Standing still. Sweating. Heart pounding. Having a panic attack on the inside. Just as scary as being lost, but knowing it would come to an end.

I heard stupid Joe Busby call out, "Got another crazy poem for us?"

"Quiet down," Principal Blakely said. "Next up, My-sty Murphy will read—sorry, that's Mysti Murphy."

We are only born with two fears. Falling and loud noises. Standing on the stage in the Beatty Middle School cafeteria isn't one of them.

I could feel all the eyes. All that heat and energy and

expectation laser-focused on me. My whole body turning red and hot and wanting to run.

I looked down and spotted Rama, smiling. And there was Wayne standing next to her, and I wanted so much for him to break the silence with some interesting fact about watermelons. But he didn't.

I searched the room for Ms. Overstreet and there she was. She nodded and I closed my eyes and thought about what she'd just told me in the hallway. "Far into the future when everyone else has forgotten this day, you, Mysti Murphy, will remember it forever!"

That was supposed to make me feel good. As if I could change my destiny by taking a stand.

And I began.

Letter To the People of Texas And All Americans in the World—

Fellow Citizens and compatriots—

I am besieged, by a thousand or more of the Mexicans under Santa Anna—I have sustained a continual Bombardment and cannonade for twenty four hours and have not lost a man—The enemy has demanded a surrender at discretion, otherwise, the garrison are to be put to the sword, if the fort is taken—I have answered the demand with a cannon shot, and our flag still waves proudly from the walls—I shall never surrender or retreat. Then, I call on you in the name of Liberty, of patriotism and everything dear to the American character, to come to our aid, with all dispatch—The enemy is receiving reinforcements daily & will no doubt increase to three or four thousand in four or five days. If this call is neglected, I am determined to sustain myself as long as possible and die like a soldier who never forgets what is due to his own honor and that of his country—Victory or Death.

Signed,
William Barret Travis
February 24, 1836

When I stopped speaking, Ms. Overstreet was standing on a chair, waving the flag of Texas. This was when I really, *really* believed I was a character in a story. I mean, if I hadn't been there myself and you had told me some red-haired seventh grader with bad teeth and too-short jeans read this letter to her nefarious middle school enemy while her teacher waved a flag, I would have said you were full-moon crazy, that does not happen in real life.

But it did.

There was silence. That loud silence I have come to hate.

But Rama and Wayne smiled at me. And even Anibal stood there blank-faced and I shot him a look of cool courage. A look that communicated, *Back off.*

Wayne shouted, "Did you know that wasn't Travis's last letter before the Alamo fell? He actually sent four more letters after this one."

And I said, "Yes, I did know that, Wayne."

I hurried off the stage and Sandy Showalter bounced up to me. "I like your friend, Mysti."

Oh brother, I thought, it's happening. Anibal gets the girl anyway. Justice isn't served. If Judge Judy was here, she would shout out, *That's baloney!* I do not want to be a mushy girl, but Anibal getting what he wants almost frustrated me to tears. I do not want to see them in the halls. I do not want to see him smile a victory smile at me in the hallways. Mostly, I do not want Sandy, who has really turned out to be nice, to be stuck with the kind of jerk who does not have much going on beneath the surface. Who is all ice and no berg. Nothing substantial lurks underneath except a certain kind of social-climbing, middle school nefariousness. I tried thinking of ways to tell her how he sleeps on a broken water bed full of stuffed animals—*Can you believe it, Sandy, stuffed animals*—and really break it to her that he might not like Taylor Swift.

But then Sandy spoke the best words to end the story. "Will you let Wayne Kovok know for me? Tell him I like him, okay? It's okay to give him my number if you want."

And I thought, Oh, sweet justice, you do exist in small corners of Texas.

chapter 43

We haven't even eaten the free Thanksgiving turkey yet, but the radio thinks it's Christmas tomorrow. Every other song or commercial is about cheer or snow or how you should be surrounded by presents.

Today I get up and make coffee for Mama. When I return to my room, I catch Laura shoving marbles under my sheets.

"I wondered when you'd grow up and try to get me back," I say.

"Oh."

"Let me brush your hair. It's a rat's nest."

"Why are you being nice?"

"Can't I just be in a good mood?"

"It's not normal."

Laura lets me brush her hair anyway. "I wonder how Christmas will be," she says.

So over breakfast, I tell Laura a story.

Laura, right as we sat down to eat a delicious dinner in which you made nice, creamy macaroni and cheese...

Ding, dong, ding.

Larry looked up at me as if to ask, Should I bark?

"It's okay, Larry," I said, and he went back to lounging.

"Who could that be?" Mama asked.

"No one nefarious, I hope," said Laura.

We all went to the door and found the Jenningses dancing on our porch.

"We've done it! The next big thing!" Mr. Jennings announced. He described in lengthy fashion how he had just that minute received the patent for the Amazing Multimeasurer and that the Home Shopping Network wanted them to sell it on TV.

"Please be our official spokesperson, Mrs. Murphy?" Mrs. Jennings asked.

"You know, when I cook, I feel so relaxed and calm," Mama said. "This is really the job for me."

Soon enough, everyone, including Mama, went to a studio in the SS Frozen Tundra, which Mama said made her feel a little less scared because we filled it with her paintings. They filmed the first-ever segment to sell the Amazing Multimeasurer.

Mama wore her pretty Cerulean Blue scarf and talked to the camera about how to mix the ingredients for the perfect bread.

"This is the cooking tool I've needed all my life!" she exclaimed with a beautiful smile.

I stood offstage watching, and then my friends Rama and Wayne showed up in a hot-air balloon because I asked them to and that's what good friends do.

Poof! They appear.

"See how good my mother is at this?" I asked them.

"I'm so glad that she wasn't doing anything else," Mr. Jennings piped up.

"Mr. Jennings, this is my friend Wayne Kovok, future inventor," I said. "He is also a fan of Steve Jobs and science."

"Did you know that sound travels about four times faster in water than air?" asked Wayne.

"Yes, I did," replied Mr. Jennings. "So, Kovok. That's a palindrome name, right?"

Woman Who Goes Somewhere strolled across the Home Shopping Network set wearing brown boots, a pink sweater, and leopard-print leggings.

"Is the fashion makeover show here?" she asked me.

Laura said, "The next block."

"Okay, thanks," she said.

After the show taped, we all had a party at 4520 Fargo Drive and ate a lot of the fresh, golden bread Mama had baked with the Amazing Multimeasurer. And then we heard the garage door open and since none of us was taking out the trash, we stared at one another and prepared for, what else, nefariousness.

And he walked in with the help of Dr. Randolph.

"Dad!" we all cried.

Dad ate bread, checked out my Alamo-in-disguise project, and then we all sat down to watch a Judge Judy marathon.

"That's a good story, Mysti," Laura says.

Hundreds of stories have propped up my bed frame. I've read a lot of them and I can tell you that all stories don't end the same way. There are sad or happy endings. Endings that keep you guessing. Endings that make you flop back on your bed and think, I guess the story couldn't have ended any other way.

That is my favorite kind of ending. Those endings have a lot in common with real life.

Now my phone beeps.

Where r u?

5 minutes

Quick, I finish making Laura a peanut butter and tuna fish sandwich and stuff it into her lunch bag.

Mama shuffles to the kitchen and kisses the top of my head.

"Have a good day, sweet girls," she says. She follows us to the front door and I hear it click closed behind me.

"I can still see you!"

"Bye, Mama."

"Bye, Mama."

Our door is Fresh Basil Green now. Mama, who can't stop painting our walls and overpainting her canvases, finally worked her way to the outside of 4520 Fargo Drive. Now our house looks the same, but different. Just like the characters who live inside it.

There is a person who paints and cooks and has joined an online support group for agoraphobics.

A person who is telling all the nurses jokes at the hospital and will be home by Christmas.

A bratty little unformed person who *still* practices raising her eyebrow as a hobby.

And a sort of courageous girl person who has a chic haircut, the ability to buy food for her family, and two good friends.

Très bon!

Rama stands at the curb, hand on her hip.

"What are you looking at? We're almost late for the bus. Hurry up!"

"Fine!"

"I have another text from Wayne."

"Of course you do. He's texted me twenty times."

"He says if we don't go to the social, he will feel awkward with Sandy and not know what to talk about and that it will destroy his future."

Well, never let it be said that Mysti Murphy helped destroy someone's future. So I say, "Okay, tell him I will go."

"You will thank me later in life."

"Stop thinking so much about what happens later in life."

"I can't. I will be a famous doctor and make the world better by curing people of cancer. You will be a famous writer and make the world better by writing about mysteries and cats with interesting names."

"It could happen," I say. "Change is coming for us all."

"That is certain."

The bus heads down Fargo Drive, traveling at the speed of change.

And that is all right.

Here is a girl who will get where she needs to go on her own two feet.

acknowledgments

It's a privilege to express thanks to those who make my writing life possible. I could not do this alone, nor would I want to. First, I'm extremely grateful to my agent, Julia Kenny. My editor, Bethany Strout, is a joy to work with, and I can't thank her enough for the enthusiasm and insights she gave to this book. Special appreciation and thanks to Alvina Ling, Victoria Stapleton, Faye Bi, and the entire talented team at Little, Brown. *Merci beaucoup* to Polly Holyoke for the generous support, guidance, and friendship throughout the writing of this book. To my amazing husband, children, and friends, abundant thanks for your encouragement and love. And finally, thanks to my Heavenly Father, who is always there to meet me in the garden when I'm in need of courage.